STRANGE SCIENCE FICTION AND FANTASY OMNIBUS

STRANGE
SCIENCE FICTION
AND FANTASY
OMNIBUS

BENSON GRAYSON

Edition September 2014

Book design by Stewart A. Williams
www.stewartwilliamsdesign.com

Contents

The Second Renaissance..1

The Washington Spring..5

Putin's Flea...11

The Mouse Who Traveled Through Time..................................17

Speak of the Devil..31

That Thing in the Cellar..35

The Man on the Moon..43

The Enemies Machine 52

Mission to Earth..56

Monkey Business 59

You Are What You Eat..62

Rocks..71

Putin for President 75

Erskine's Law...80

SNAFU..84

The Cat's Meow...87

Homo Superior 102

The Perfect Drug 105

Limbo 109

Precepts of Statesmanship 124

Civilization? 126

Admiralty Affairs 133

Double Indemnity 136

Bancroft's Time Machine 141

The Enigma of Washington 145

Eat up no More 149

The Devil You Know 152

The Vulcan Project 157

Obesity 165

The Seers 169

The Sterling Prize 174

Mad Scientist 178

Avoid the Fire 184

Follow the Rats 187

School Reform 191

The Probe 195

The Submersible 200

Halloween 206

The Second Renaissance

The rebirth of knowledge of the ancients, known as the Second Renaissance, originated in Washington, D.C. in the middle of the Twenty-First Century. Its geographic location was associated with the fact that the Library of Congress, in the nation's capital, had become the largest single repository of copies of the works of the ancients. This status had been conveyed upon it by the fact that the original documents had been destroyed during the ravaging of the libraries of Europe in the first and second world wars.

The immediate cause of the Second Renaissance was the decision of the Library of Congress to copy all of its extensive holdings into a newly installed cloud computing system. The intention was to help preserve them from deterioration, and to enhance the Library's capability to make the contents readily available to users around the country. During the work of preparing the holdings for uploading to the computers, some of the library staff happened to look at the documents, and were intrigued by what they found. They were astounded to learn that the commonly-held belief that the earth is round, and that it orbits the sun were relatively recent, and that for the greater part of man's existence, it was understood that a flat earth is orbited each day by the sun.

It was impossible to contain the news. Word of the discovery traveled rapidly among the library staff, and subsequently to outsiders. It became a hot topic of discussion in Washington political circles and along Embassy Row. Some prominent scientists, unwilling to see their scholarly reputations unravel, dismissed the new findings as an absurd superstition. They might conceivably have been successful, if they had not been publicly challenged by a few of the more progressive graduate assistants, and junior professors.

A re-examination of the "proof" that the earth is round revealed that most of the claims to have circumnavigated the earth were due to navigational blunders. The apparent evidence that the earth is not flat, offered by individuals clinging to that obsolete theory, was shown to be pure fable when it was explained that a slight elevation in the center of the flat earth, which gives it the shape of an upturned saucer, accounted for the appearance of the masts of a ship before the entire vessel comes into view. Further proof became available when the U.S. Navy radio station in Guam found, in its files, a copy of the last radio transmission of the lost aviator, Amelia Earhart, on July 2, 1937, stating that she "had reached the end, and that her plane was falling into the void," a clear reference to having flown off the rim of the world.

A crucial event aiding the spread of the new learning, came when the Massachusetts legislature voted to require textbooks used in the state public schools to include material drawn from the ancient texts. Other states quickly followed suit, with only a few holdouts in the Deep South.

The most rapid changes, as a result of the Second Renaissance, came in the areas of politics and government. The ancients had clearly shown the inefficiency of the democratic system. When carefully examined by the unbiased mind, it was clear that giving every person the right to vote, regardless of their intelligence, interest, or ability would produce results far less efficient than a limited franchise. Systems of weighted voting, or limiting the ballots to those over forty-five, were tried and found wanting. So too, was rule by an oligarchy. Eventually, by general consensus, it was decided to appoint a king for life.

Initially, there were some attempts to limit the power of the King. These were successfully rebuffed, by citing the frequent references in the ancient documents to the divine right of Kings. Obviously, when the Almighty himself selected the proper individual to be king, it was feckless for ordinary mortals to challenge his wisdom.

A logical byproduct of the adoption of an absolute monarchy was the establishment of a state church. It was correctly observed, that it made little sense to suffer the disputes among various denominations, over the technical points of doctrine. Only one religion was correct, and who better to decide on religious dogma, and head the church, than the king himself?

From the political and religious sectors, the new doctrines spread to include economics. Capitalism and the free market, all economists had to agree, led to widespread waste and inefficiency. New firms kept on being established, taking on heavy infusions of cash, only to go bankrupt in the inevitable cycle of boom and bust. The obvious solution was to go back to the wisdom of the ancients, combining as many firms as possible into giant monopolies. The success of this new policy was proven, when all of the competing telephone companies were re-combined into a giant American Telephone and Telegraph Company, which was given a permanent monopoly position over the nation's telephone sector. Millions of Americans cheered, when the restored telephone monopoly reinstated the long-valued abilities of subscribers, to learn the time and weather, via a simple phone call.

Medical science similarly benefited, aided by the discovery that the so-called "germ theory" had been concocted by the Fenwick Pharmaceutical Company in 1897, in an effort to promote the declining sales of their products. As Dr. Amadeus Foster asked, when he accepted the Nobel Peace Prize for Medicine, "How can people possibly believe in a germ, which they can't see with their own eyes?" Most scholars today credit the advances made in modern medicine, to the precept taught in scientific classes at all levels, primary, secondary and university, that no matter what the theory states, if you can't see it, it doesn't exist.

It is hard for many of us living today to believe that our ancestors clung so foolishly to superstition, and ignored the advanced knowledge of the past. Probably the most important thing we can teach our children, is to avoid the error of discarding past beliefs for whatever fad achieves temporary popularity.

The Washington Spring

It all began in Washington, D.C., in the capitol of what was once the most powerful nation on the globe. As with so many important movements in history, the incident causing it was quite trivial. Jonathan Smith, a twenty-seven year old "yuppie", working as a deputy assistant to a section chief at the Treasury Department, returned home to his efficiency apartment, in the prestigious northwest area of Washington, and found a letter from the Civil Service Office stuck in among the advertisements in his letter box.

Opening the envelope, Smith found it contained a notification that his monthly paycheck had been increased by twenty-three percent,; three percent as his annual in-grade step increase, seven percent for a merit pay bonus, and thirteen percent to cover an increase in the annual rate of inflation; the official figures having been carefully adjusted to disguise the fact that the real rate of inflation was more than double that. This good news, regrettably, was more than counter-balanced by a fort-seven percent reduction in his net pay. This depressing result, according to the Civil Service Office, stemmed from a ten percent increase in the annual tax rate, a twenty-three percent increase in his cost for mandatory life insurance, and fourteen percent surtax to cover the medical insurance made available to individuals who could not otherwise pay for it.

Smith gulped as he read the notice. This was the fourth year in a row that his net salary had actually gone down from the year before. As an intelligent man, he reached the logical conclusion. His life would only become worse. There was only one possible solution - suicide. Turning to the conventional methods of doing away with oneself, Smith carefully considered poison, hanging, and slitting his wrists. None of these seemed attractive. All were distinctly unpleasant.

Having an inventive mind, Smith found the perfect solution. The next morning, he visited four of the public health clinics in Washington that dispensed heroine in small doses to addicts, under a plan to gently wean them off the drug. By slightly disguising his appearance at each clinic, he was successful in obtaining doses at all four clinics. He then returned to his apartment, and settled down to expire. As he had never before used the narcotic, or any dangerous drug, the result was foregone.

What would otherwise have resulted in no more than a brief notice on the obituary page, was drastically altered by Smith's careful preparations before the deed. Not only did he mail letters to all major newspapers in the northeast describing his dilemma and his solution, but he also prepared a movie for you tube, in which he discussed his situation at length. All four of the TV networks immediately seized the opportunity for a human interest story in their nightly news shows, three of them going so far as to omit coverage of the ongoing civil war in Syria, so as to expand their coverage of Smith's tragic suicide.

Nationwide, the popular response to the story of Smith's fate was immediate. Many individuals tied yellow ribbons on their fence posts, and letter boxes as memorials. Men wore yellow ties, women yellow scarves. Some yuppies, identifying themselves with Smith, likewise committed suicide. A few, however, recognizing that suicide was a permanent step, elected instead to resort to looting. This was not only better at relieving their inner tensions, but also could be monetarily advantageous.

Being yuppies, most of the looters were selective in what they chose to loot. Few stores had imported bottled water in their windows, and imported handbags were of little use if the color was not right. Therefore, they began to think of a more satisfactory method of displaying their outrage at the way American culture had declined in recent decades, and hopefully, of effecting a change.

The defining moment came in early April. George Burrows, a youngish economist at the Commerce Department, walked to Lafayette Square Park, just across from the White House, climbed on to a park bench, and began speaking. Other government staffers, also crossing the park on their way homeward, saw him and began to listen to his words. Burrows excoriated the U.S. government for the widespread favoritism, corruption, and duplicity. But his harshest words were directed at the way of life of the average American. He called upon men to shave off their beards, to cut their hair only in the crew cut style familiar to Marine Corps, and to dress only in three-piece suits, with starched white shirts, and striped ties. Women, he demanded, should raise the hem of their skirts to a minimum of six inches above the knee.

Burrows' revolutionary message spread across the country, and many heeded him. Hundreds of his followers camped permanently in Lafayette Square, living in tents and parading along Pennsylvania Avenue with signs, calling upon the government to resign. All of this was widely covered by television, which helped the movement to spread. Social media and the internet fostered the revolution abroad, first in Canada, and Great Britain, but subsequently in places as distant as Tibet and Bulgaria. Burrows' followers, of course, could always be identified by their revolutionary style of dress, as prescribed by Burrows.

The aftermath of the events in Washington that Spring, was initially peaceful. Not all of those involved in the movement, however, shunned violence to accomplish their aims. Clandestine groups formed and began to obtain arms. They were not united under a central organization, but cooperated in working for a common purpose. Most of them adopted the umbrella name of United Servants of America, customarily abbreviated to USA, which evoked feelings of patriotic loyalty among its adherents.

Washington, and virtually all other governments around the world ignored the growing danger, regarding it as a temporary phenomenon. The potential threat of USA become apparent a few months later, when a private yacht approached the coast of Morocco, and brought a small force of USA's. Most of the thirty odd revolutionaries were from the United States, but their number included volunteers from Canada, Great Britain, Norway, and Brazil. All the men were dressed in their uniforms, three piece suits, white dress shirts, and striped ties. The three women among them wore the short skirts demanded by their ideology.

The USA military campaign was brilliantly directed. The landing spot, just south of Morocco's largest city, Casablanca, was not guarded by any government security forces, so that the invaders could debark unhindered. Unfurling their black banners, they then advanced northeast toward the Moroccan capitol of Rabat.

News of the invasion rapidly spread, and Moroccan troops were dispatched to stop it. Despite greatly superior numbers, the invaders had little difficulty in continuing their progress, aided by massive defections from the Moroccan Army. Many Moroccan soldiers shed their uniforms, donned the three piece suits of the invaders, and joined their ranks. This was true even more with regard to the Moroccan officer corps, many of whom had secretly been seduced from their loyalty to the King of Morocco. by the thought of being able to wear their hair in a crew cut style, and by a desire to see their wives and sweethearts in miniskirts.

Rabat fell to the invaders after the briefest skirmishing, the defenders melting away or joining the revolution. Around the world, USA groups, both overt and clandestine, hailed this success. In sudden, unexpected strikes, USA adherents seized power not only in Baltimore, Maryland but also in Manchester, England, and Halifax, Nova Scotia.

The fall of Baltimore to USA militants raised concerns in world capitals that the threat to existing order was potentially deadly. The manner of USA's treatment of the population of Baltimore, the most important city yet under USA sway, was considered to be a litmus test of their intentions. Initially, USA ruled with a light hand. No sooner had the city, and its surrounding area been brought under full USA control, then the situation changed radically.

Males who refused to shave their beards, adopt the crew cut style haircut, and don three-piece suits, were summarily executed on the spot. Women fared no better. Crew cut USA warriors broke into private residences, and questioned all women they found as to why they were home, rather than working in an office. Any women whose skirts were deemed too long had the garments cut off far above the knee. As a clear signal to all who saw them that they had sinfully violated Burrows' doctrines, their eyebrows were ruthlessly shaved off. Perhaps the greatest barbarity, was the case of some fifty odd females found at home, who were dragged out at gunpoint, loaded aboard packed vans, and carted to Harvard University, where they were obliged on pain of death to study for graduate degrees.

As news of these events flashed around the globe, the various world leaders reacted in characteristic fashion. In Washington, D.C., the President rejected suggestions that he add USA representatives to his Cabinet, instead ordering his security forces to use fire hoses and tear gas to drive USA supporters that had been camped in Lafayette Square. A significant number of the government troops, revolted by this deed, shed their uniforms and deserted to the USA. USA troops slowly encircled the American capitol, raising fears in foreign quarters that Washington's defenses would collapse.

British Prime Minister David Cameron, stung by the loss of Manchester to USA, charged that British security was being eroded by the influx of illegal immigrants, via the Common Market countries, and ordered the tightest controls on immigration since the end of World War II. The reaction was not limited to the Western nations. The Iranian President made an emergency trip to Israel, where he urged the Jewish State to forget its difficulties with Iran, and join in a common effort to combat the USA menace. which was threatening both nations. As an added inducement, he suggested the two nations should jointly cooperate in the development of nuclear weapons. Similarly, Russian President Vladimir Putin, and Ukrainian President Petro Poroshenko, whose nations had been less troubled by USA attacks, due to concentration on other internal matters, flew together in Putin's personal jet to Washington, where they unsuccessfully urged the American President to broaden his government.

If the loss of Baltimore, Manchester, and Rabat to the USA was unexpected, the USA takeover of New York City was even more so. The residents of that metropolis awakened one morning to see the black USA banner flying above all government buildings. Journalists who questioned the residents of New York City, about their reactions to the takeover, were told, only in private, that New Yorkers certainly did not agree with all USA ideology, but preferred it to that of the government in Washington.

As the world now waits apprehensively, to see if the USA will somehow be contained, or if it will grow to encompass the entire globe, it is too early to reach a definite conclusion. That will have to be the work of later generations of historians. All that can be concluded at this time about the events of the Washington Spring, is that the forces that shape the course of civilization are often determined by trivial events.

Putin's Flea

Russian President Vladimir Putin was not a happy man. It is true that he held in his own hands more power than that exercised by the Tsars in the last years of the Romanov dynasty. It is also true that not only did he control vast resources as president, but he could obtain as much more as he might desire by applying pressure to the oligarchs who dominate the Russian economy. And of course the Russian Federal Security Service, the domestic replacement for the former KGB, could be counted upon to eliminate ny opponents he could not intimidate or bribe.

Still he had his problems, he was well aware that if too many of the oligarchs combined against him, he might have difficulty in prevailing over them. Similarly, he also had to carefully monitor the personnel of the internal security apparatus to ensure they remained completely trustworthy. He even had to consider somewhat the attitude of the West, since access to Western markets and capital made it easier for him to expand the Russian economy, and strengthen his popular support. But the thing that troubled him most was the lack of anyone he could completely trust.

Musing on this problem one day, the Russian President recalled something he had seen in a recent Hollywood movie about Washington politics. One of the characters had said, "If you want a friend in Washington, get a dog." Putin suddenly realized this was the solution to his problem, he would get a dog. As president, he had no difficulty in implementing this decision immediately. One of his aides brought in several suitable candidates for the position of presidential dog, and Putin chose one, a Russian wolfhound, whom he called Pushkin, after his favorite Russian author.

Pushkin quickly came to occupy an important place in Putin's affections. The dog was given his own bathroom in the Kremlin next to Putin's office. He slept on Putin's bed at night, sat at his feet at the dinner table, and traveled with Putin in his limousine each morning from Putin's residence to the Kremlin. His diet consisted of prime quality steaks accompanied by such tidbits from Putin's dinner table Pushkin chose to consume.

As he sat at his desk studying state documents sent to him, trying to decide which policy option would be the most effective; Putin occasionally would talk to himself. One day as he did so, Pushkin looked up at him and began barking loudly. Putin was shocked; this was not typical of the dog's behavior. Then it dawned on him. Pushkin was laboriously trying to communicate with him via Morse code. Putin grabbed a pad and .transcribed the dog's comments. He realized Pushkin was giving him advice in response to the problem the president had raised while talking to himself.

Putin looked at Pushkin's words and decided that the dog had given him sound advice. He followed it and everything went perfectly. Naturally, the Russian President began to discuss all his problems with Pushkin and follow the dog's guidance. Since he was completely sure of Pushkin's loyalty and intelligence, there was no reason to do otherwise. Naturally, it was too unwieldy to have lengthy discussions concerning complex matters with Pushkin via Morse code. Putin devised a system to phrase his side of the discussion with the dog as simple yes or no questions which Pushkin could answer briefly with one bark for yes and two for no. Everything went well.

Then one day everything changed. Putin asked his canine advisor the best tactic to use in dealing with a planned opposition political demonstration against his holding another term as president. The dog barked once and Putin therefore ordered the internal security service to crush the planned rally. This decision proved to be most unfortunate. Many of the demonstrators were injured and a few killed as a result of the heavy handed tactics employed by the Federal Security Service. A storm of criticism of Putin and of the Russian government erupted around the world, and the Western nations were provoked enough to temporarily impose measures which slightly reduced the profits of the major Russian corporations.

Putin shrugged his shoulders over the incident. His faith in Pushkin's advice was not in the least diminished and he continued to depend on his policy recommendations. A few days later, the situation was repeated. Pushkin's suggestions as to the proper course to follow in dealing with a major American petroleum corporation also turned out to be wrong. Did this weaken Putin's dependence on the dog for advice? Not in the least.

Although Putin entertained no concern over these events, the same could not be said for the Federal Security Service. Its chiefs knew they were in bed with Putin. If his increasing number of policy failures caused a lack of popular backing for the Russian President, it could reach a point where he would be ousted. And if Putin were forced from power, he might be replaced by a ruler who would reorganize the internal security apparatus and remove the current leadership. Naturally, this was a calamity to be avoided at all costs.

The internal security apparatus secretly began a detailed surveillance of Putin and of Pushkin. After some time, its officers discovered the problem. Pushkin had a flea. When the flea bit him, Pushkin became distracted and devoted all his attention to removing it from his tender parts. At such moments, Pushkin could not give the necessary attention to what Putin was telling him. If the Russian President was unfortunate enough in his timing to pose a question while the dog was scratching, he would give the first answer that popped into his mind, usually one bark for yes.

Having ascertained the problem, the internal security chiefs had to come up with the proper solution to this delicate problem. They knew that it would be too hazardous to discuss it openly with the Russian leader. Therefore, they summoned the best field operatives from the Russian Foreign Intelligence Service, their old colleagues from the days before the Soviet KGB was dissolved. The elite officers selected for this activity were the Foreign Intelligence Service chiefs in Washington, London, Bonn and, Beijing. The four officers flew to Moscow to discuss and jointly come up with a solution.

The four went over the delicate problem, but could not arrive at a common solution. Some favored assassinating the dog, others assassinating the flea. They even brought in from Bulgaria a top agent they had employed to kill some political figures with an implement camouflaged as an umbrella, whose tip injected a poison which left no discernible trace in the victim.

As it happened, while the discussions were under way, the Foreign Intelligence Service chief in Malta, who had been back in Moscow on vacation, happened to pass by the room and overheard the discussions. He was a relatively junior official and did not have much of a reputation with the senior security officials. But he was extremely clever.

The Malta chief knocked at the door and entered before he could be ordered to keep out. "Comrades," he said, as he had been taught to call his superiors during the Soviet era, "I could not help but overhear your problem and I have the perfect solution."

"What is it?" they cried in unison, forgetting this breach of protocol in a desire to have the answer to their dilemma.

"It's simple," came back the reply. "Don't assassinate the flea. Turn him into a double agent. We keep him in place and feed him the answers to give to Putin. Not only do we prevent Putin from getting the wrong advice, we give him the answers that are best for us."

"That's a fine idea," said the chief from Washington. "But how do you recruit a flea?"

"Aha," came back the answer from the Malta chief, who had not the least idea. . "I certainly can't reveal to you the tactics I've employed with so much success in Malta to secure excellent flea agents. It would violate all of the basic security rules. And you comrades have no need to know."

The four chiefs had to agree with this statement. They gave the Malta chief a week to handle the problem. They didn't have to spell out the details about what would befall him if he failed: not only he, but his entire family and all of his friends and neighbors would be sent to work in the Siberian mines for life.

Well aware of his opportunity and also of his peril, the Malta chief set out furiously to solve his problem. With careful surveillance, he determined that the flea was happily married and returned home each night to his wife. The flea had no known weaknesses and was a faithful husband.

Fortunately, the Malta chief was up to the task. He recruited the most voluptuous female flea courtesan, who was susceptible to large bribes, with the promise that her father would be released from a Siberian labor camp if she succeeded. It was arranged that she would encounter the flea on his way home to his wife after leaving Pushkin. She used all her wiles on the flea. He found himself in her room making love with her. He was unaware that all of this was being recorded by a hidden camera.

The flea had his pleasure with the courtesan and went home to his wife, feeling embarrassed by his behavior. He felt even worse when the next day he was picked up by two internal security officers and taken to their headquarters. Shown the embarrassing photos, graphically illustrating his adultery with the flea courtesan, and informed these would be shown his wife unless he agreed to cooperate fully, he had no choice. He was a broken flea. He agreed to become their agent, body and soul.

Today, Putin contentedly goes on following Pushkin's advice.

The dog by and large gives sound advice to the Russian leader. Occasionally, the flea is instructed to bite Pushkin when the internal security service wishes him to take a course they believe best.

The former Malta chief has been recalled to Moscow and given two quick promotions. He is now a senior officer in the Federal Security Service and occupies an office next to the Russian President. His sole task is to operate "Operation Flea" as the project is referred to in the intelligence service books. Because of his knowledge of what the flea will do, he has established close personal ties with Putin and is widely expected to be the next chief of the Federal Security Service. And, on another happy note, the courtesan flea's father was released from the Siberian camp and is now happily residing with his daughter in Moscow.

The Mouse Who Traveled
Through Time

It is generally believed that only the human mind is sufficiently complex to formulate the concept of time travel. This is not entirely true. Among the many who fruitlessly attempted throughout history to create a time machine, one individual actually succeeded. He was, surprisingly, not a human, but a member of the species mus musculus or, in ordinary English, a mouse. Ludeveccio, the mouse in question, was born sometime after 1140 A.D. in what was then the Kingdom of Sicily. Its ruler, Roger II, was a descendent of the Normans who left Scandinavia in the Tenth Century in search of a more favorable environment and managed to find their way through the Straits of Gibraltar into the Mediterranean Sea, and then to the island of Sicily. The Norsemen found it easy to conquer the island. Under Roger II, who succeeded in unifying the various Norman-controlled parts of Sicily into one Kingdom, agriculture and trade with the Arab lands to the east, flourished.

Ludeveccio had the good fortune to be born and grow up in the palace of King Roger II. His father had died early in his infancy as the result of an encounter, while inebriated, with a palace cat, and so the young Ludeveccio and his siblings were raised exclusively by their mother, Maria. The latter was extremely intelligent and Ludeveccio along among his siblings inherited her intelligence and then some. His mother was an excellent provider, furnishing her young with all manner of delicious cheeses, obtained during the night from the palace larder. As a result, Ludeveccio did not have to devote his time to searching for food. Each evening, he spent his time listening to the wise men who counseled the King and his Court. The adolescent Ludeveccio found himself particularly fascinated in the discussions of mathematics and science, many of them based on the knowledge of the ancients which had been preserved by the Arabs and which had been carried to Sicily by travelers.

Ludeveccio's life changed for the worse in 1154, when Roger II died and was succeeded by his son William I, known in history as William the Bad. The loss of the foreign territories conquered by Roger II caused a lowering of the general standard of living. This was particularly felt in the palace, where Maria now was barely able to feed herself, let alone her children. Ludeveccio's siblings departed Sicily one by one, on ships headed for other countries in the Mediterranean, hoping to find greater opportunities there.

Ludeveccio, however, was too prudent to embark for a foreign destination without some knowledge of what he might find there. When Maria succumbed to old age and Ludeveccio finally concluded that he, too, would have to leave Sicily, it was too late; the number of vessels setting out from Sicily had been severely diminished. No matter. Ludeveccio was certain that his brilliant mind and the knowledge of advanced science and mathematics he had acquired would enable him to find a solution.

In this, Ludeveccio was not mistaken. Why not create, he thought, a device that would not only transport him out of Sicily to a place of greater opportunity, but also through time, to a period in which living conditions for mice were more favorable. The exact nature of the machine he fabricated has been lost in history, but it most definitely worked. On a dismal fall morning, so Ludeveccio later remarked, he mounted the time machine and set off.

The device fabricated by Ludeveccio actually worked! Within a few seconds the intrepid mouse found himself leaving the soil of Sicily and flying high over the waters of the Mediterranean. It must be added, however, that the time machine did suffer from some defects. It could be turned on and stopped, but it contained no controls for the speed at which it traveled, either through space or time, and no means of knowing whether it was traveling into the future or into the past. There was a rudimentary steering mechanism, consisting of a sail, but it blew off because of strong gusts of wind, as Ludeveccio flew over the Straits of Gibraltar and into the broad Atlantic. It was not that Ludeveccio had been unaware before he commenced his epic-making trip of these flaws in the device's design. Rather, he had knowingly sacrificed efficiency in the interests of speed of construction.

Ludeveccio was further handicapped by his ability to judge his time in the air. The sun was moving to rapidly in the sky for him to make accurate solar observations and the wrist watch had not yet been invented. After an unknown period, part of which the mouse was asleep, he awakened and saw he was once again over land and slowly descending in altitude. Beneath him he could see an unending land mass, covered with trees, occasionally some dessert, and one long and high chain of mountains.

Finally, Ludeveccio got a glimpse of water bordering a strip of sandy coastline. As he neared the water, he could see that it was vast, quite possibly another ocean. All this was, of course, new to Ludeveccio. He possessed a good knowledge of the charts and maps available in Twelfth Century Sicily, but none of them covered much beyond Europe, the Near East and the northern part of Africa.

The time machine gently touched down on the sand, close to the water, as though it was being guided by a divine hand. Ludeveccio stepped on to the sand. It was warm under his feet, but felt good after the cold of the higher altitude at which he was been travelling. He had not the slightest idea of where he was or whether he had traveled into the past or the future. Still, conditions were probably better than they had been in Sicily. Certainly, the ruler would have to be better than William the Bad.

Ludeveccio set fearlessly in search of some mouse he could ask. None were anywhere in sight. The sole occupants of the beach appeared to be large seabirds, who were interested in dining on fish rather than mouse and paid him no interest.

Some distance down the beach, ludeveccio spotted something dark lying at the water's edge, washed over by the encroaching tide. As he neared it, he realized it was the body of a human lying face down, only the head still uncovered by the waves. At first he thought it was dead, but realized as he watched it that the person was still breathing.

Ludeveccio's first inclination was to leave the human in the surface where he had found it and proceed on his search. As his mother had taught him, it's a wise mouse who does not stick his nose into matters which do not concern him. However, Ludeveccio's tender heart came into play. He was certainly not as pious as his mother, Maria, had been, but he still entertained the belief that a merciful God would overlook his occasional lapses and permit him one day to enter Mouse Heaven. He reversed his steps and returned to the body. The tide had advanced further in just a few minutes and only the back of the body's head still protruded from the water.

It was clear to Ludeveccio that the body was far too large and heavy for a small mouse to move on his own. Ludeveccio walked rapidly to the side of the head and saw an ear exposed. He bit it gingerly, hoping to awaken the human. No result. He bit harder. The body quivered, nothing more. Desperate measures would have to be applied.

Ludeveccio step back for a minute to muster all his strength and then bit the ear as hard as he could. The body sat up and the head turned to face him. Slowly it opened its eyes. They were as red as any eyes the mouse had ever seen. "Wash the matter?" it asked.

Back in Sicily, Ludeveccio had acquired a smattering of many foreign languages from the conversations of the foreign traders he had overheard at the palace. This man, that the human was male was a conclusion he reached from its deep voice, seemed to be speaking a form of archaic English.

"My name is Ludeveccio," he said. "I am a stranger here. I come from Sicily."

"Ishaly? Where's that?" asked the man. When he spoke, his words were accompanied by a smell of hard liquor.

So that was the matter, Ludeveccio concluded. The man was not sick or injured, just highly intoxicated. Ludeveccio never indulged in hard spirits, himself, cautious not to repeat the fate of his later father, who had been killed while inebriated. Still, many of the humans in the palace had overindulged, and Ludeveccio had been a silent observer of their behavior.

"What's your name?" he politely inquired of the man.

"Dishney," came back the answer, in another gush of strong alcoholic breath.

"Well, Dishney," Ludeveccio began, speaking as distinctly as he could so that the befuddled human might understand, "don't you think it would be better to get out of the surf? ".

In response to the mouse's urging, Dishney clumsily struggled to his feed and began a lumbering walk away from the surf toward a line of cottages that bordered the beach, Ludeveccio struggling to keep pace. He appeared to be wearing some gray, two piece cloth garment, with a white patch showing toward the top of his jacket. The wet material hung down and he looked much like a walking scarecrow.

After a few steps, Dishney fell to his knees, exhausted by the effort of walking. "Please, please get up Dishney," the squirrel implored. The man started walking again, a little faster. Then, he stopped, seeing that the mouse was falling further and further behind. He stooped, swaying a bit, gently enclosed Ludeveccio in a giant fist, and inserted him into a compartment in the jacket, only Ludeveccio's head protruding.

Dishney finally reached the beach cottage he had apparently been steering toward. He extracted a key from another compartment in his lower garment and fumbled for several moments, attempting to place it into the lock. After numerous failures he grasped the hand holding the key with his other hand and managed to turn the door lock and enter the house. Inside, the human collapsed across a bed on the far side of a room. Ludeveccio feared that would be crushed as the man's body hit the bed. Fortunately, Dishney remember in the nick of time that he had the mouse in his pocket and managed to twist to safeguard his companion from the force of the fall.

Almost immediately, Ludeveccio heard loud snoring emanating from the human. Dishney had fallen asleep, still clad in his wet garments. The mouse carefully extricated himself from the garment and looked around the room. He thought of exploring it, but decided he was too fatigued. It had been a long and tiring day. Ludeveccio found on the floor one of Dishney's used stocks and curled up comfortably in it. Within seconds, he too was asleep.

Ludeveccio was awakened by the clattering of dishes. He opened his eyes. The room in which he slept was empty, but through the doorway he saw Dishney in the kitchen. He was drying dishes, stopping every minute or two to drink from a cup. The mouse walked into the kitchen and climbed to the top of a small table.

"Good morning, Dishney," he said curiously. His mother had always instructed him to be polite.

The human dropped his cup, which shattered on the floor, spilling a dark, tan liquid.

"My God!" he said, almost hysterical. A talking mouse! I must have the DT's."

"Come, now," said Ludeveccio" is a calming voice. "Don't you remember? I saved your life yesterday by persuading you to get out of the water, when you were lying face down in the ocean."

"So that really happened," the man said. "I thought it had to be a drunken dream. I knew I shouldn't have bought that bottle of gin. I just can't handle it."

Ludeveccio felt embarrassed. He really shouldn't have reminded Dishney of his sorry condition of the day before. To change the subject, he said "I'm feeling a bit hungry. Do you happen to have any cheese in your house?"

"I apologize for my poor manners," the man said. "I've been a poor host. Please sit down and I'll see if I have any cheese in the house."

Dishney walked to a large, white metal cabinet along one wall and opened a door in its front. A white light came on and Ludeveccio could see various foodstuffs in its interior. The man removed an orange block of what appeared to be food, cut off a piece and placed it on a saucer, which he set before Ludeveccio.

"I'm afraid all I could find was this American cheese," he said. "I do hope you like it. Would you care for something to drink? I have coffee ready and there are some bottles of soda in the refrigerator."

"If I may, just give me some water," the mouse answered. He had no idea of what coffee or soda were and was a bit apprehensive about trying strange foods. He bit into the so-called American cheese and had to hide his disappointment. As hungry as he was, he found it difficult to eat. It was certainly not like any of the Italian cheeses he enjoyed.

Then he noticed that Dishney had taken another cup from the counter and poured more of the coffee into it. He then added a white liquid which looked like milk.

"Is that cream?" Ludeveccio asked. "If it is, may I have some to drink?" Dishey poured some of the cream on to a saucer and placed it on the table in front of Ludevecchio.

"Thank you, Dishney," the mouse said politely.

The man frowned. "Do you have difficulty in pronouncing Disney?" he asked. "My name is not Dishney. It's actually Walt Disney."

Ludeveccio felt foolish and turned a beet red. His mother had always instructed him to take pains to learn the exact name of the people to whom he had been introduced and to make certain he pronounced it properly.

"I'm so sorry, Disney," he said.

"I gather from your manner of speaking," the human said, "That although you speak it rather well, English is not your native tongue. "It's improper here to refer to someone by just their last name. It implies a feeling of superiority. "I would prefer it if you would call me Mr. Disney or, if we become friends, as Walt. "

"Of course, Mr. Disney," Ludeveccio said,. not wishing to appear pushy by calling him 'Walt.' My name is Ludeveccio. My mother only gave me one name. My father's name was Medici, he added proudly. He was from one of the most distinguished families in Florence."

"I'm glad to meet you Ludeveccio," Mr. Disney said. "Tell me, you said your father came from Florence. Is that Florence, Italy?"

"Why yes, of course." He recognized the use of the name Italy, although generally it had not been used in Sicily. "Can you tell me where we are? I've been traveling, and when I met you on the beach I was actually uncertain of my location.."

"We're in southern California, close to Hollywood."

This did not make sense to Ludeveccio. He had a good knowledge of geography as it was known back in Sicily, but clearly he was a considerable distance from his home. Possibly, he could ascertain in what time he was in. Not wanting to mention the time machine, he decided to probe the subject indirectly.

"Do you know which day it is?" he inquired.

"Why yes, it's April Seventeenth," Mr. Disney said.

This was of no help. "I wonder if you could tell me the full date, including the year. As you noted, my English is not as good as it should be, and I'd like to be able to use it correctly."

"Of course," Mr. Disney said. "It's April seventeenth, nineteen twenty-eight."

Nineteen twenty-eight. Ludeveccio realized that he had traveled almost eight hundred years into the future.

"My God," Mr. Disney suddenly exclaimed, putting down his cup of coffee. "I almost forgot. I have a meeting today with the studio. I have to get dressed and be there by ten." He hurriedly put his cup on the table and started to get dressed. "I have to make a good impression," he said. Ludeveccio was unsure if Mr. Disney was talking to him or to himself. "But what can I tell them?" he asked. "I still don't have any good idea in my head."

Ludeveccio was sorry Mr. Disney was so agitated. "Can I help you?" he asked. "I wish you could, Mr. Disney" said sorrowfully. I've been trying to think up a story line for a cartoon full length cartoon movie. I just can't think of one. That's why I was so drunk yesterday. I've just become so depressed."

"Let me try," the mouse answered. His mother had always told him to offer a helping hand whenever needed. "It would help me I understood what you mean by cartoonist and movie."

"I forgot you're not from Hollywood," Mr. Disney said thoughtfully. "I forgot you're from Italy. I guess they haven't developed cartoonists or movies there. A cartoonist," he explained, is a type of artist. Only he doesn't draw exactly how a person looks but exaggerates some feature, usually to make his drawing humorous. Such as making a man's large ears even larger or a man's sharp nose even larger. A movie," he went on, "is a series of pictures showing movements, each one a little bit later in time, drawn so as to give the impression of the person shown moving. The word is actually a contraction of the name, moving pictures."

"I think I understand," said Ludevecchio. But why do you want to make fun of a person by exaggerating some flaw in his appearance?"

"Generally, we draw cartoons of political officials, to show our disapproval of their actions or policies. Occasionally, we may draw a cartoon of an animal, such as the lion to represent the British Empire. The problem is I've been asked to propose a cartoon movie about an animal. I can't think of what animal to use or what the story line would be."

"That doesn't seem an insurmountable obstacle," the mouse answered thoughtfully. "I suppose under some circumstances, some people might consider me to be an animal. I would be pleased to assist you by serving as a model for a cartoon. Nothing really exciting has ever happened to me, but I have a good imagination and could probably suggest a story line or two."

Walt Disney looked as though an inspiration had just hit him in the face. He grabbed a sketch pad and charcoal, eyed Ludeveccio for a minute, and then began drawing furiously. When he finished he showed the mouse what he had drawn. It was of what appeared to be a mouse, but one standing up on his back legs. Ludeveccio had occasionally taken that position, but it was not really comfortable for him. The mouse's ears also far too big, Ludeveccio supposed in an effort to make it amusing. It was really difficult, the mouse thought, to understand the human sense of humor. Probably, the oddest part of the cartoon was that Mr. Disney had dressed the mouse in a short garment covering his legs down to the knees, gloves and shoes. Since mice are protected by their fur and do not need garments the way humans do, Ludevecchio assumed this also was supposed to be funny.

To be polite, Ludevecchio smiled and nodded his approval. He hoped that Mr. Disney was a better judge of human humor than he was. Mr. Disney then took back the pad and carefully colored the sketch, using water colors. The mouse in the sketch was colored the same as Ludeveccio's own fur, but the gloves were white, the shoes yellow and the pants green. Once again, Ludeveccio yielded to Mr. Disney's superior knowledge of people.

Mr. Disney finished dressing, put the sketchpad into a briefcase, and walked to the cottage door. "Wish me luck, Ludevecchio," he said. If I can't sell this to the studio, we're both going to be out on the street. The door closed and the mouse began pacing the floor, in a state of great apprehension. From time to time, he would try to divert himself by climbing on to the table and staring out at the beach and ocean. To no avail. Each second was an hour, each hour an eternity.

By studying the position of the sun through the cottage window, Ludeveccio realized that it was now late afternoon, and Mr. Disney had still not returned. He prayed that the human had not become so depressed at having his proposal rejected that he had gone out and gotten intoxicated again. The mouse was also frightfully hungry. If he could have been sure of opening without breaking it the large metal cabinet Mr. Disney had referred to as the refrigerator and securing more cream, he would have done so, though he certainly would not have eaten any more of that awful stuff Mr. Disney called American cheese.

When he was on the brink of going out on to the beach and seeing if Mr. Disney was lying down in the surf drunk, he heard the cottage door open. Mr. Disney entered a gigantic grin on his face. "We did it!" he explained. "The studio loved the idea. They signed me to a great contract and gave me a big cash advance. How can I ever thank you? Naturally, we'll split the cash fifty-fifty."

"There's no need for that, Mr. Disney" the mouse replied. "After all, what's your success is my success. All I ask is that you give me a good home and feed me good cheese and cream every day."

"That goes without saying," Mr. Disney replied. He opened a paper bag he had I his pocket. "I could tell you didn't care for the American cheese," he said. "The reason I am so late is that I tried to buy some good Italian cheese for you. None of the stores I tried had any. I was about to give up when I passed one of new Italian restaurants that have opened up. I entered and explained my problem. The chef was most helpful. He sold me a bit of a cheese he called pecorino. When I said I had never heard of it he explained that it is made from sheep's milk and is very popular in Sicily.

Mr. Disney sliced a bit of the cheese and put it on a saucer in front of Ludeveccio. The mouse tasted it and smiled. It was the best cheese he had had in a long time. Back in the happy days when

Roger II was king of Sicily, the mouse had occasionally had the opportunity to gather a piece or two of it. The cheese brought back the happy days he had passed at the palace.

Mr. Disney, meanwhile, had removed his sketch pad from the brief case and opened it for Ludeveccio. "The studio," he explained, generally liked my idea, but made a few suggested changes. Under the circumstances, I thought it was wiser to accept them all. I'm afraid they thought your fur not colorful enough and proposed I make it black. Similarly, they didn't like your shorts colored green and wanted them to be black, with yellow buttons. Is that acceptable to you?"

"Of course," Ludeveccio answered. He certainly didn't want to call Mr. Disney any trouble.

"I'm afraid there is still one other change," Mr. Disney said carefully. "I didn't like it. If you wish, I will go back to the studio and try and get them to change their mind." From his demeanor, the mouse could sense Mr. Disney hoped he wouldn't have to take this step. Ludeveccio wondered what horrible disclosure Mr. Disney was about to make.

"Naturally," Mr. Disney continued, "I proposed we call the hero of the cartoon Ludeveccio, after you. They objected. Said it was too foreign. Then I suggest Medici, after your father. They liked that better, but still thought it too foreign sounding for American audience. They anglicized it to Mickey and want to call the hero Mickey Mouse." Ludeveccio, thought for a minute. "I agree," he said quietly.

The rest is history. The first Mickey Mouse cartoon proved to be a great financial success and many more cartoon movies and comic strips featuring the mouse followed. The cartoon studio bearing his name flourished and he became a multi-millionaire many times over. Today is still exists as one of America's largest companies. Walt Disney and Ludeveccio move to a grand new home Walt Disney purchased in Hollywood, although they kept the little beach cottage for vacations.

Walt Disney and the mouse became such good friends that Ludeveccio began referring to Walt Disney by his first name and he affectionately called the mouse by the nickname Lou. Every day, Ludeveccio dined on the finest of Italian cheeses and he slept every night in a little bed, on satin sheets. As a treat for the mouse, when time permitted, Walt Disney would carry Ludeveccio concealed in his jacket pocket to the Pasadena campus of Cal Tech, where he would drop the mouse for the day. Ludeveccio would go to one of the seminar rooms used by the advanced engineering and physics classes to audit the discussions, concealing himself behind the books in a bookcase. On several occasions, when the professor mistakenly declared there was no possibility of time travel, Ludeveccio was tempted to voice his objection. However, he always managed to hold his tongue, aware that humans do not take kindly to being corrected by a mouse.

He mouse lived a very long and very happy life. At last, as it must to all mice, death came for Ludeveccio. As the end drew near, Walt Disney took Ludeveccio to the little cottage on the beach, and placed the mouse's bed on a table so that he could look out and view the beach and ocean he loved so well. On Ludeveccio's final night, Walt Disney did not leave his side, holding Ludeveccio's hand and softly weeping. He did not want to say goodbye to his best friend, to whom he owed so much.

Shortly after dawn, Ludeveccio opened his eyes to take a last look at the beach and ocean. The sight was always dear to his heart. It brought back the memory of his arrival in California and his meeting with Walt Disney. Closing his eyes, he said more to himself than to Walt Disney, "I have had the most wonderful life any mouse could possibly have. I now pray that the most merciful God will permit me to enter Mouse Heaven. He then breathed his last, an expression of complete satisfaction on his face.

There is only one sad footnote to the story of Ludeveccio's life. His time machine, the only time machine ever invented on this earth, vanished from the beach on the day of the mouse's arrival,

washed away by the tide. The machine, which could have contrib-
uted so much to human knowledge, now sits on the ocean floor
some miles off the California coast. It was last viewed by human
eyes in 1948, when a diver came across it while checking on an off-
shore oil drilling platform. He actually picked it up and examined
it. Owing to the advanced state of deterioration and its tiny mouse
size, he failed to appreciate its potential value and deposited it on
the ocean floor, where it remains to this day.

Speak Of The Devil

The shade of John Wilkes Booth was unhappy. This was not surprising. The souls of the damned in Hell are supposed to be unhappy. But the shade of the late actor was so unhappy that it aroused attention. One day, Satan sent for him.

"You're giving Hell a bad name," he declared. "You're supposed to be miserable here because of the punishments we inflict. Instead, you're making yourself unhappy. That's against all the rules and I urge you to brace yourself and cheer up. Let us be the ones who make you unhappy."

The damned soul of Booth looked even more sorrowful at these words. "I'll try to do what I can," he said, "But I don't think it will do any good. I'm just so miserable."

Satan's nonexistent heart was, of course not touched. Still he was interested. "What seems to be your personal trouble?" he inquired.

"I was a great Shakespearean actor," Booth said. "But today, nobody remembers that fact. All they think about is that I assassinated Abraham Lincoln."

"Well after all, you did do that," came back the Arch Fiend.

"O.K., O.K., so I did do that," admitted Booth. "One little mistake. Everyone makes mistakes. Lincoln wasn't very nice to his wife Mary," I recall. "And I believe that as a lawyer, he got several murderers acquitted by fooling the jury. Anyhow, they named a monument after him. Nobody has ever named anything after me."

"Well what do you expect me to do about that?" demanded Satan. "Nobody ever claimed that life is fair. Are you hoping I will give you a pass to Heaven? Don't be foolish. Take your medicine like a man. Follow the proper procedures, and let us make you as miserable as your deeds in life require."

Satan's words did not have the desired effect on Booth. Instead the late actor began a lengthy soliloquy from "The Merchant of Venice."

More to shut him up that anything else, Satan asked, "Do you have any practical remedy to suggest?"

"All I want is a chance to defend myself," Booth said with a hangdog air. "Why don't you let me post a clarification of my story on a bulletin board in Hell?"

Eager to end the conversation, and wishing to ward off another Shakespearean soliloquy, the arch fiend agreed. "Just write out what you want to say, and I'll take a look at it. As long as it sticks to the facts, it should be acceptable."

Both expressed their thanks and left. Booth did not return for some time. Naturally, he was not excused from the daily round of tortures inflicted routinely on the souls of the damned in Hell. When he reappeared at Satan's office, he handed the Devil the draft statement justifying his actions, and waited expectantly.

The arch fiend looked at the draft and whistled in admiration. "John," he said, marking the first time Satan had ever referred to a denizen of Hell by his first name, "We have a lot of advertising geniuses here, but you are by far the best."

And the draft written by Booth was indeed impressive. It began by referring to the fundamental religious and political authorities. The Bible, it noted, teaches that only someone who is without sin should cast the first stone, and that no one should judge, lest he be judged. The treatise repeated the famous words of the Magna

Carta in 1215, that one is entitled to a trial by a jury of his peers, and to the French Bill of Rights of 1789, that everyone is presumed innocent until proven guilty. How could he be blamed for Lincoln's assassination, Booth pointed out, when he had not been properly convicted by a jury of his peers, for the deed?

The draft then emphasized that Booth was the victim of a poor environment, being born out of wedlock, with his mother the mistress of Booth's already married father. The late actor was further suffering from doubt over his self image, saying at times he was an Episcopalian, and on other occasions admitting he was secretly a Roman Catholic.

Finally, it turned to describing the virtuous life booth had led, except for that one admittedly unfortunate transgression. Abraham Lincoln, it noted was widely commemorated, with a city in Nebraska named after him, as well as his face appearing on the U.S. penny coin, and the five dollar bill, not to mention an imposing monument in his honor in the nation's capitol. This was the same man, Booth continued, who had violated the American Constitution during the Civil War, because he supported, until quite late in the Civil War, the continuation of slavery, in those American states in which it was legal. He concluded by reminding the reader that he also frequented prostitutes before he was married, and after his marriage, was believed by his wife to be treating her shabbily, and as defense attorney, hoodwinked juries into acquitting obviously guilty murderers.

"My boy," the Devil said, "How would you like to assist me to improve my image? We have rather a serious problem with the way most people look at me, and at Hell. I'd like you to prepare an advertising campaign for me."

The campaign Booth prepared for the Devil more than met Satan's expectations. Booth was given a private office next to the Arch Fiend, and has free access to him. Naturally, he has not been officially exempted from the usual torture of the damned souls, but he is subjected to it only to the extent that it does not interfere with his advertising work. Of course, Booth makes certain that the advertising functions take up all of his available time.

The first phase of Booth's advertising campaign is already in full swing. According to a public opinion poll, in 2013, only forty-three percent of all Americans believe the Devil really exists. As the actor's shade pointed out to Satan, one cannot be alert to the Devil's lures, if he does not believe he exists.

That Thing In The Cellar

Jimmy Peterson was a bright little five year old boy living with his parents in a small Ohio city. His father was the star reported on the local daily newspaper. Jimmy's mother had taught school before he was born, but now stayed at home caring for him. As a school teacher, she was especially good at dealing with children and Jimmy was exceptionally bright and outgoing for his age.

Then one day Jimmy's father was offered a job as a copy editor on a large paper in Washington, D.C. Times were hard, the salary offered was most generous, and Jimmy's mother was expecting another child. With only the slightest of regrets, Jimmy's father accepted the offer and the family moved to the nation's capital. Now they found it difficult to obtain a suitable residence. Although they had sold their old home in Ohio, they found housing prices in Washington much higher.

Although Jimmy's father enjoyed his new job, he thought of returning back to Ohio. Fortunately one day, the family learned of a home for sale within their price range. When the real estate agent took them to see the property, they were astonished. It was an old Victorian mansion, four stories in height with a peaked roof and turrets. It occupied a large wooded lot far from the closest neighbors, whose houses could not be seen from the mansion because of the high trees surrounding the property. When they the agent the reason for the surprisingly low price for the house, he explained that it was owned by an estate that wanted very much to dispose of it quickly.

There was no reason to delay. Although the mansion suffered from neglect with the windows boarded up, it would be worth many times the offering price once a few moderate repairs were made. Accordingly, the family purchased the house and moved in. It was so large and had so many rooms that the furniture they had brought with them from Ohio did not begin to fill it. Jimmy was given his room on the third floor, one floor above his parents' bedroom.

The move from Ohio seemed to have changed Jimmy. He was no longer the cheerful, outgoing child he had been in Ohio. He missed his old friends and his comfortable old home. His mother gave birth to a daughter and had to devote most of her time to caring for the infant. What time she could spare from that had to go to her housekeeping chores, which greatly expanded due to the many rooms in the mansion. Not only did Jimmy no longer have the full attention of his mother, he now had no children to play with because the house was so isolated.

Whenever Jimmy attempted to persuade his mother to play with him, she shooed him outside. There he found the vast shaded lot depressing. Playing inside was even worse. Many of the rooms were empty and the floors covered with dust. He hated his own bedroom because it seemed so isolated. Trying to sleep in it at night was even worse because of the strange creeks and sounds he occasionally heard. When he told his parents about them, they scoffed at him, telling he was a big boy now and should dismiss such childish fears. On one occasion when he had been awakened suddenly by the noises, he ran to his parents' bedroom and pleaded to be allowed to share their bed for the night, only to be most curtly refused.

One rainy day Jimmy decided to try the cellar. He had had only a brief glimpse of it through the open cellar door when they moved in and thought it might be warm and cozy because of the boiler located there. Turning on the cellar light, he slowly descended the stairs. The light bulb was very dim and much of the cellar remained in shadow. Along the ways he saw the outline of crates, large and small and of broken furniture. In one corner, he beheld a spinning wheel of the kind he had seen in one of his picture books.

Suddenly he glimpsed movement in the shadows. Some vague shape seemed to move. Then he saw what he believed to be two large yellow eyes staring directly at him. Then heard a loud crash, which could have been the boiler starting up. Petrified, he turned and ran up the stairs, slamming the cellar door shut behind him.

Running for safety to his mother, he found her in the kitchen feeding the baby. He blurted out what he had seen and pleaded sobbing for her to protect him. Irritated at the slamming of the door, which had upset her daughter, Jimmy's mother rebuked him coldly, chiding him for being so foolish. When he refused to be calmed, she gave him a smack on the cheek with the back of his hand and ordered him to go straight upstairs to his room and stay there.

Jimmy's father returned that evening from work and found his wife still furious about Jimmy's behavior. Normally a patient man and very fond of his son, he was tired after a hard day's work and feeling stressed by the need to learn a new job. Going upstairs to see Jimmy and hear him explain what had happened, he was as deaf as Jimmy's mother to the story of a dangerous thing hiding in the cellar. When he was unable to talk Jimmy out of his delusion, he finally lost his temper too and gave his son the first spanking he had ever received.

Jimmy, once a cheerful, outgoing child, became increasingly sullen and morose. He stayed outside the house all day regardless of the weather and had to be dragged inside to eat. In desperation, his parents took him to a child psychological, who tried to cure him of his obsession. When that failed to cure Jimmy he was taken to other child psychologists, including several who recommended the parents going with Jimmy into the cellar and showing him that there was no dangerous thing hiding there. They did so, but despite the absence of any untoward thing in the cellar, Jimmy refused to be convinced.

Jimmy's parents next tried taking their son to a psychiatrist specializing in childhood disorders. All agreed that Jimmy was extremely bright but suffering from an unshakable obsession which if not cured could result in series mental illness. One even mentioned the alternative of a lobotomy, very rarely used except in the most extreme cases.

Jimmy's parents were seriously considering institutionalizing Jimmy when his maternal grandparents stepped in, offering to take their grandchild into their home. The grandfather had owned a small farm in Ohio. He was now semi-retired, renting out most of his land but still keeping a small heard of dairy cattle. His parents gratefully yielded up their troublesome son, and he was taken back to Ohio by his grandfather, who had traveled to Washington to escort him back to the farm.

Jimmy never saw or heard from his parents or sister again. Under the sympathetic care of his grandmother and grandfather, he rapidly regained his old sunny disposition. He did very well at school, had many friends and enjoyed helping his grandfather tend the cows after school.

A few months after starting school, Jimmy returned to the farm and found his grandparents sitting in the living room. His grandmother was weeping, and his grandfather is looking very grave. When he entered, his grandmother rose and hugged him. "Jimmy" he heard his grandfather say gravely. "I have something I have to tell you."

His grandfather placed him on his lap. "Your parents and sister have all been taken by God," he said softly, kissing him on the cheek."

Despite this tender age, Jimmy recognized the awful meaning of those words. "You mean I will never see them again?" he asked, seeking to confirm his understanding. "Not until you meet them again in Heaven," his grandfather answered. Jimmy began to sob, and then abruptly stopped. The happy memories of his parents he had from his early childhood days in Ohio were crowded out by the loathing he had felt toward the Washington move. Added to this was the attitude his parents had displayed toward him about that thing in the cellar.

Under the benevolent care of his grandparents, Jimmy grew to be a fine young, very devoted to them and regarding them as his real parents. When he grew a bit older, Jimmy asked his grandfather to tell him what really happened to his parents. The older man answered that had only been informed that the entire family had been found murdered in their home, that no motive had ever been ascertained and that the killings were still kept on the books by the Washington police as an unclosed case

Jimmy graduated from high school and left the farm to attend college. He initially planned to major in agriculture and return to help run and eventually inherit has grandfather's farm. However, he did so well in English that several of his professors suggested he switch his major and go into writing as a career. After some consideration and recalling that his father had enjoyed being a reporter, he decided to do so.

Upon graduating from college, Jimmy worked for a year to live with his grandparents, working in the nearby town as a teller in the bank to save enough money to pay for graduate work in journalism. With his savings and part time work, he was able to complete journalism school and took a job at a local Indiana weekly. From there he moved as a reporter to the Indianapolis paper, where he was considered a top reporter and was considered, but did not win, a Pulitzer Prize for a highly-praised series of stories on corruption in some state agencies.

Jimmy's reputation was so good that he received an offer from the "New York Times" to join its staff, and he thereupon moved to New York. He married an attractive, intelligent young woman from the Mid West who worked in the paper's business office, and they had two children. Everyone who had a chance to observe Jimmy's behavior toward his children remarked that he was the most attentive, caring father they had ever seen.

Some years later, the newspaper asked Jimmy to go down to the nation's capital for a few weeks to assist in its Washington Bureau. He normally would have been reluctant to go notwithstanding the opportunity this afforded to have him permanently assigned to work there because of his reluctance to be apart from his wife and children. However, his wife was planning to go with the children to stay for a short time at her parents' beach cottage so that the short assignment in Washington would not constitute any real hardship.

His arrival in Washington marked the first time he had returned to that city since his leaving it with his grandfather as a child. For more than a week, he worked out of the Times Washington Bureau, enjoying the experience very much. One day, when he happened to be passing the offices of the "Washington Post," he decided to go in and check the old files of the paper to see if it had published account of his parents' murder. He had earlier tried to do so with the microfilm copies of the "New York Times" issues for the period but could find no mention. This he didn't regard as unusual, after all the Times would not normally cover a murder in a city some two hundred miles away from New York.

Since he had a general idea of the date his grandparents had first told him about his parents' fate, it was not too difficult for Jimmy to find and read the story. It was rather a long one on the first page of the section dealing with city events. He learned that the police had discovered the bodies, alerted that something might be amiss by his father's paper, which reported that he had not turned up at the office for several days and that the phone had apparently been left off the hook.. The victims were not only murdered.

The story referred to the bodies of the victims being torn apart and mangled as though by some wild beast. It added that the police had been forced to break into the mansion as all doors and windows had been securely fastened from the inside. There were no signs of any attempt at forced entrance and no indication that the murders had resulted from a botched robbery attempt.

So sensational were the murders that follow-up stories about it appeared on succeeding days. .Many of the facts from the original story were repeated, along with statements from the police that no motive for the crimes could be uncovered. The story on the third day told Jimmy something he had no seen before. The paper had uncovered the fact that a very similar still unsolved crime had taken place in the mansion some six years before, An entire family including three small children had been brutally murdered, with the victims' bodies torn apart and mangled beyond description. Following the earlier crime, the house had been boarded up and left uninhabited. Prospective purchasers, it added had been discouraged by the violent crime that occurred in it and because of the gossip in the neighborhood that it "was haunted."

After work, Jimmy on a whim hired a taxi to take him to see the mansion. It was fortunate that he had copied down the address. When he arrived at the site, he found it completely changed. The mansion had been razed and all of the tall trees cut down. Where his parent's home once stood, he saw eight very modern town houses occupying the lot.

When his assignment to the Washington Bureau was over, Jimmy carefully warded off suggestions by the Bureau Chief that he might wish to become a permanent member of its staff. He departed Washington by train as rapidly as he could, heading for the shore to spend the weekend with his wife and children at his in law's beach cottage. Jimmy never returned to Washington again. He was always very grateful he had not learned whether had been his imagination or if he had really glimpsed something horrible in the mansion cellar. It was something it was better not to know. But of one thing he was absolutely certain. He was very glad he had refused to let his parents convince him he had not seen anything there and that one of the most fortunate days of his life was the day he left with his grandfather to return to Ohio.

The Man On The Moon

Herman Hawthorne was unique in two distinct areas. He was the third richest individual in North America, thanks to his late father's early investment in the shale oil industry. Secondly, he was the world's worst curmudgeon. Hawthorne cared not one iota for the opinions of other people. Everyone except him, he said often and loudly, was either a fool or a charlatan, or both. Naturally, he could hardly be said to be well liked.

None of Hawthorne's views were widely accepted and most were almost universally discredited. His claims that the germ theory had no basis of fact but was actually invented by the Pinnacle Pharmaceutical Company in 1904, in what was a highly successful campaign to increase the sales of its drugs was universally scoffed at, despite Hawthorne's proof that a high percentage of all pharmaceutical products are today actually purchased by individuals responding to widespread television advertising. Similarly, his assertions that earthworms actually do fall from the sky when it rains, rather than simply fleeing their flooded homes was flatly denied by all reputable scientific bodies, notwithstanding Hawthorne's clear evidence that no widespread scientific research had ever been conducted to objectively look into his theory.

Hawthorne was born and raised in northern Florida, far from

the family's holdings of shale oil leases but close to the bank, to which all the royalties from the shale oil operations were funneled. As a child, Hawthorne was taken by his father to observe one of the space shuttle launches at Cape Canaveral and this incident made a lasting impression on him. Not a favorable impression. Even as a child, Hawthorne distrusted what anyone told him and thought the so-called space shuttle launch was a giant fraud.

Growing to adulthood, Hawthorne's greatest campaign was aimed at proving that NASA's statements about space exploration were all part of a giant hoax, designed to illegally obtain funds by whichever corrupt administration was in power in Washington. "Can you honestly believe," he would assert to all who would listen, "That we actually sent a manned expedition to the moon? Why even Jules Verne's novel A Trip to the Moon is more creditable."

Hawthorne was so certain of his derogatory opinion about NASA that he decided to obtain the necessary proof. There were fewer obstacles to Hawthorne attempting to do this than for most other individuals because of his great personal wealth. But even for a person with Hawthorne's resources to replicate the American space program would have been too costly.

Fortunately, Hawthorne had other arrows in his quiver. Alone among prominent Americans, Hawthorne had strongly endorsed the Russian annexation of the Crimea. Ignoring popular outcry, he further loudly identified himself with Moscow's call for Ukraine to cease its effort to join the European Economic Union. Russian President Vladimir Putin was so grateful over this rare show of foreign support for his policies that he sent a warm, personally hand-written note to Hawthorne, thanking him and inviting him to visit Russia.

Hawthorne quickly accepted the invitation and travelled to Russia. In Moscow, he was treated with the same ceremony as would be accorded a friendly head of state. At the formal dinner in his honor, he was seated at the table next to the Russian President, and he and President Putin spent almost two hours in friendly conversation. It was during this meeting that Hawthorne extracted from Putin a promise that Russia would permit him to use its space facilities to send his own expedition to the moon.

The Russian President probably did not expect he would have to honor his promise to Hawthorne. After all, of what use is a commitment to use Russian space facilities if one does not have a space capsule. Hawthorne had no official backing so there was no practical chance of his buying or borrowing a space capsule. Undaunted, Hawthorne thanked Putin, departed Moscow the next day and back in the United States began furious efforts to obtain a space capsule. With his great wealth, it was still difficult but not impossible.

After examining his options, Hawthorne heard of an ex-Air Force Major and former astronaut, Harley Mathews, who had been forced out of the program after a series of highly-publicized extra-marital affairs. The one-time astronaut had NASA Training to pilot a space capsule. Mathews was now in bad financial shape, attempting to eke out a living as a salesman of aluminum siding while paying large alimony payments to his former wife, and providing child support to the unwed mother with whom he had fathered a child.

Hawthorne contacted Mathews and offered him a six-figure salary and two year contract if he would agree to head the proposed expedition to the Moon. His duties would include designing a capsule for the journey and then piloting it. Despite the great temptation of the financial package, Mathews truthfully explained the many practical obstacles in the way of such a project. His objections were dismissed and Mathews agreed, assuming that Hawthorne would come to realize the futility of his plan and abort it, but not before Mathews would receive a healthy cash infusion.

Without further delay, Hawthorne purchased a closed auto manufacturing plant in Michigan and installed Mathews in an office on the top floor, formerly housing the factory management. From his office, Mathews could observe the work of the labor force on the factory floor below. Mathews' first task was to draw up the plans for a space capsule capable of transporting a crew of two from the Earth to the Moon, landing on the Moon's surface, and then safely returning the crew back to Earth.

Initially Mathews just went through the motions, aware of the apparent futility of the project. He was astounded when Hawthorne asked to see the plans, carefully inspected them and then gave Mathews detailed instructions on how to improve them. Mathews realized that although Hawthorne was eccentric, he was nevertheless extremely intelligent and had good technical knowledge.

The finished design was for a space capsule resembling in appearance a rustic log cabin. Despite its odd appearance and its smaller size than the space capsules designed by NASA, it was theoretically possible for it to reach the Moon. In some respects it was even better. Mathews was aware, from personal experience in piloting a space capsule, of defects he could now correct. He now employed new technology and material developed since the original space capsule design was finalized. Its thrust engines were more powerful than earlier ones and capable of extreme speeds, despite the relatively heavier weight of Hawthorne's capsule, due to the reinforcing of its sides to prevent damage from collisions with dust particles in space.

The plans completed, it was now time to begin the manufacture and assembly of the various component parts. Some were to be manufactured in the plant, others to be obtained from outside suppliers. Hawthorne showed great skill in supervising the award of the contracts. He was aided by the fact that he did not have to employ certain companies as suppliers that had powerful advocates in Congress, nor was he obliged to purchase from the lowest cost bidders who might actually be unable or unwilling to supply the highest quality item.

Mathews had no difficulty in assembling a trained work force, being able to choose from among the many unemployed workers in the area. The space capsule was completed ahead of schedule and shipped to the East coast to be loaded onto a fast merchant vessel chartered by Hawthorne to transport it to a Russia Black Sea port. When the ship neared its destination, Hawthorne and Mathews flew directly to Moscow on Hawthorne's private jet.

Russian President Putin was surprised and annoyed by Hawthorne's arrival. He was deeply involved in handling the crisis with Ukraine, seeking to keep that country within the Russian orbit while avoiding a rupture with Western Europe and the United States. He never anticipated when he made his vague commitment to Hawthorne that he would actually request the use of the Russian space facilities to send an expedition to the Moon. Putin therefore invited Hawthorne to tea at the Kremlin, planning to spend only a few minutes with him and then return to more important matters.

Their meeting did not go as the Russian President had planned. Hawthorne not only voiced his strong endorsement of all Russian actions toward Ukraine, but volunteered to repeat them at a news conference in Moscow and again in Washington. Putin was particularly overjoyed by Hawthorne's declaration that "If he had been in Putin's shoes, he would react just as Putin had reacted." A public statement like this from one of the most powerful American business leaders would clearly aid Russian propaganda and greatly bolster Putin's standing in Western Europe.

Unsurprisingly, the Russian President quickly agreed to Hawthorne's request for help with his expedition. Putin issued instructions for Russian officials to accord every possible assistance and to treat the proposed launch to the Moon as the equivalent of a top priority Russian project. When the vessel transporting Hawthorne's space capsule docked, it was unloaded promptly and sent by rail to the Russian space launch facility at Baikonur in Kazakhstan. After his press conference, at which he repeated the statements on Russian policy toward Ukraine which he had told Putin, Hawthorne and Mathews were flown on Putin's personal jet to Baikonur.

The lift off a few days later went according to plan. Mathews, extremely nervous and not certain that the capsule would actually survive in space, found that when he took control it functioned perfectly. The capsule and its two man crew enjoyed an uneventful flight to the Moon with everything going well except for Hawthorne's stomach, which rebelled at the feeling of weightlessness in space. At the critical moment when the capsule was to land on the Moon's surface, Mathews did an excellent job, executing a smooth landing.

As soon as the ship stopped moving, Hawthorne rushed to dress himself to begin his exploration. He had equipped the capsule with only one protective suit, seeing no reason why Mathews needed to leave the ship. Giving Mathews instructions to prepare for a return to Earth as soon as he returned, Hawthorne went through the airlock and stepped down onto the moon.

Hawthorne did not expect to spend much time on the moon. He was quite sure that he would learn enough in a few minutes to confirm his suspicion that no human had ever actually landed on the moon, and that all accounts to the contrary had been fabricated for ulterior purposes. He felt much better even in his confining space suit than he had during the trip, his stomach having returned to normal.

Notwithstanding the heavy space suit, Hawthorne made good progress, aided by his much lighter gravity on the moon. He ascended a small hill and then saw in front of him a depression in the surface, about twelve feet deep and probably some thirty yards long and wide. In the center was a large circular mound. The height above the mound declined on a gentle gradient and Hawthorne was able to walk down it with no difficulty.

Nearing the mound, he changed his mind about it. It did not look like a hill and in fact like something not naturally made. Could it be a house? His mind rebelled at that thought. Circling the mound he saw what might be a door. Feeling very foolish he approached it and knocked. The door swung open. Inside Hawthorne saw a human type figure. At first glance, it appeared to be his own height, but when looking down he realized it was floating about a foot in the air. It was wearing some type of white garment and emitted a type of soft radiance.

"Are you a Moon Man?" Hawthorne asked, hardly believing his eyes and feeling very foolish in asking.

"Don't be idiotic!" came back the answer in perfect English. "What else could I be? Do you really think I might be a Martian?"

Hawthorne was taken aback. He was pondering what to say when the Moon Man went on. "You might as well take off that helmet you're wearing around your head. There is plenty of oxygen in this depression for you to breathe properly."

Feeling he was taking a dangerous risk, Hawthorne unscrewed his helmet, removed it, turned off the oxygen supply coming from the tube mounted in the back of his space suit, and took a breath of the air. It was surprisingly fresh.

"You see, "said the Moon Man triumphantly. "Now sit down and make yourself comfortable.

Hawthorne sat down on what looked like a chair. Apparently the Moon people did not always float in the air but availed themselves of furniture. "Would you care for some Moi?" The Moon Man asked, speaking more politely than before. Before Hawthorne could answer, he poured a thick, viscous red liquid from a flask into a metal goblet and handed it to Hawthorne. The visitor from Earth tasted it, found it surprisingly refreshing and downed the contents.

"What is this?" he asked. "I didn't think you could grow anything on the Moon."

"We can't," came back the reply. "Moi is an organic compound manufactured in the molten core of the Moon and forced up through cracks in the surface of depressions such as the one in which I am living. That's the way we get our oxygen as well. Forced up from the core. I believe our Moi may be similar to the manna referred to in your Old Testament as being furnished by your God to help the Israelites survive in the desert."

Hawthorne was amazed that the Moon Man knew so much about events on Earth and spoke such colloquial English. When he inquired, the Moon Man explained that the inhabitants of the Moon regularly listened to radio broadcasts emanating from the Earth. "We also receive your television signals," added, "But they are usually too scrambled for us to make much sense of them. Additionally, we learned your language when we sent exploratory missions to Earth many centuries ago. We decided at that time you were too primitive a species for us to have any interaction with, always concentrating on murdering each other, and that in the future we should do all that we could to prevent you from learning of our existence."

"If you actually visited the Earth," Hawthorne asked, "Why is there no record of it in our history?"

"Actually, there is," came back the answer, which left Hawthorne even more confused. "Many of your accounts of ghosts represent human sightings of us. If you think about it, you can see our appearance is rather similar to the descriptions of ghosts."

Remembering the purpose of his mission to the Moon, Hawthorne said. "I am very glad to have made the trip here and to have met with you. I always suspected that all the reports of NASA expeditions reaching the Moon and exploring it were fabricated. If they had really done so, they would have encountered you or other Moon People and reported that to Earth."

"You're being foolish again," the Moon Man said reproachfully, "they didn't see us because we deliberately concealed our existence from them. It's a simple matter to camouflage our depressions and our residences so they are indistinguishable from the Moon surface."

Hawthorne realized that he had spent considerable time speaking with the Moon Man and that it was necessary for him to leave and return to the space capsule. "One last question," he said. "Since you Moon people have taken such pains to avoid Earthmen learning of your existence, why have you revealed yourself to me?"

"That's very simple," came back the answer. "There are three reasons. In the first place, if you told the people on Earth what you have seen and heard, they would not believe you. You would be confined in a mental institution. The second reason is that if they did believe you and sent another mission here to look for us, we would simply conceal our existence, as we did during your previous Moon walks. Of course, the third reason is the most important."

"And what is that?'" Hawthorne blurted out.

"It's just this. You are never going back to Earth. You are here permanently."

"What do you mean?"

"Go to the door and look out." explained the Moon Man.

Hawthorne rushed to the door and opened it. High in the sky, disappearing from sight, he beheld the spacecraft returning to Earth. He cried out in horror and began cursing, then sobbing. In a few minutes, however, he regained his composure. Actually living permanently on the Moon with the Moon people would not be that bad. Their Moi was pretty tasty fare. If he stayed here, he would not have to undergo that awful feeling of weightlessness again. But best of all, if he stayed here, he would be dealing with a species much more rational, more intelligent and nicer than what he had observed on Earth.

The Enemies Machine

The multi-million dollar super computer dubbed the "Enemies Machine" was constructed under the direction of the Advanced Research Project Agency under the overall supervision of senior Pentagon officials. Once built, the CIA and other members of the Intelligence Community played the major role in providing data to be inputted into it. It belonged to the first generation that can properly be said to think. Much like the human brain, its circuits were wired so that rather than just being limited to pulling up individual pieces of data, it was able on its own to recombine them in every possible combination and then provide the most logical answers to the questions asked of it.

The project was started on the orders of some of Washington's top policy makers. The members of the President's National Security Council believed they were handicapped in dealing with various word crises by the incorrect advice they were receiving from the intelligence community. Intelligence analysts, even those with the deepest knowledge of a foreign country, tended to base their predilections on what that nation's response to U.S. moves might be to their own view of the universe. In other words, they were unable to view anything from the perspective of the foreign leaders. While this admittedly reflected a good deal of Monday morning quarterbacking, the President believed the "Enemies Machine" would provide a useful adjunct to the existing National Security Council apparatus and authorized expenditure of the required funds.

The "Enemies Machine" was seen as providing the solution. Into its data banks were imputed all of the many separate items of information bearing upon the geography, history, culture, society, economy, political structure and religion of the various countries. Because of the then limited capacity of the computer, not every nation in the world could be included. Therefore, the database was limited to only the ten nations considered most likely to be involved in a serious world crisis affecting the U.D. These included Russia, China, North Korea, Cuba, Iran, Saudi Arabia, Afghanistan and Iran. In the light of later events, the most significant omissions were Syria and Venezuela. Another shortcoming was the failure to consider Ukraine as a nation separate from Russia.

To enhance the accuracy of its estimates, the machine was given a brilliantly designed internal map projection capability, so that its responses were based on the geo-strategic viewpoint that would be those of the host populations and their leaders. Since in virtually every country of the world maps prepared in that country show it as the center of the world, this was the underpinning for the machine's analysis.

The first test of the computer was and after the fact re-examination of the probable Iranian reaction to the ouster of Iranian Prime Minister Mohammad Mossadegh in a coup involving the United States. It correctly predicted the popular furor caused by the overthrow of the democratically elected leader and the likely build up of a violently anti-American sentiment. This analysis so pleased the president that he ordered henceforth U.S. actions in any world crisis be based on the readout from the "Enemies Machine."

The first test of the machine in real-time came when American policymakers considered re-orienting the thrust of U.S. policy away from Europe and the Middle East to give the situation in the Far East the highest priority. When the machine was asked to provide the probable response to the so-called "pivot" in policy, it responded with a prediction that the Chinese Communist Government would interpret the move as a deliberate American provocation revealing a hostile intent in Washington. No American offer of increased military cooperation with China or public expression of good will would convince Beijing otherwise.

Shortly thereafter, the pro-Russian President of Ukraine Viktor Yamukovych was forced from power by public demonstrations in Kiev by agitators favoring close association of the country with the European Community, the "Enemies Machine" was asked to provide analysis of the probable Russian reaction. The answer was that Russian President Putin would never accept this as fait accompli but would resort to whatever tactics required to keep Ukraine from slipping out of the Russian economic orbit. Neither Western promises of continued good will toward Russia nor threats of economic sanctions would induce the Russian President to abandon his goal.

These analyses were submitted to the National Security Council, which did not know what to do. If accepted as accurate predictions, they would require a significant change in the direction of American foreign policy. Could or should Washington abandon its traditional goal for every U.S. foreign policy initiative? How could the Washington political establishment countenance abandoning its firm belief that the establishment of popular democracy in every nation of the world, regardless of the level of education, standard of living, hostile attitude toward the U.S. or religious fanaticism deserved the highest priority for the long term, regardless of the scope of unfavorable results in the short and medium term?

The problem was deemed too important for the National Security Council to decide, and so it was taken directly to the president. The Chief Executive weighed the issue carefully, carefully considering all aspects. Then he made his decision. The traditional all-out drive for global world democracy could not be reversed nor even modified in the smallest degree. He ordered that all documents referring in any way to the recommendations of the "Enemies Machine" be shredded and burned. To prevent any future re-occurrence of such obviously unsound estimated, he decreed that the machine be destroyed along with all documents relating to its design or use.

Today, the citizens of the United States and indeed of the entire world can rest easier in their homes. They know that no considerations of national self-interest or of common sense will be permitted to intrude into American foreign policy.

Mission To Earth

For several decades astronomers on Ganymede, the largest satellite in the solar system one of the moons of Jupiter, had trained their most power telescopes on earth. The reduction in size of the earth's polar icecaps led the astronomers to conclude an intelligent civilization on earth was diverting the water from the icecaps to supply massive hydroelectric projects. Some astronomers asserted that the occasional white flashes that they observed came from the launching of spacecraft; they were more widely believed to result from the impact of meteors hitting Earth's surface. At length, the government decided to construct a spaceship that could travel to Earth and enable a scientific team to examine the earth's surface minutely and confirm if possible whether there was any intelligent life there.

The actual decision to fund the project, however, was not based on scientific interest. Rather it was due to substantial pressure for the program by leading defense firms on Ganymede, who saw in it an excellent opportunity to increase their profit margins At length the spacecraft was finished and the crew members chosen. It was launched from Ganymede with a cascade of publicity and lengthy speeches from leading politicians.

Because of the length of the journey from Ganymede to Earth, even with the high propulsion engines of the spacecraft, the crew members would not remain awake for the entire journey. After it was in orbit, and the course set, the automatic pilot was put in operation, and the crew members carefully arranged themselves in closed capsules, took the necessary drugs, and went into a condition similar to hibernation. Many decades later, the crew members were awakened. Climbing out of their capsules, the pilots turned off the automatic pilot and resumed control of the ship.

The spacecraft entered Earth's atmosphere at very high speed. The arrival had been times to occur during the hours of darkness to lessen the likelihood of its being observed by any intelligent life on Earth. The ship's velocity slowed and settled down softly at the designated landing spot. After examining their instruments, the crew determined that the atmosphere of Earth would not sustain them outside the ship and that they would be obliged to conduct their examination of the surface protected by spacesuits.

All of the crew wished to walk personally on the surface of the Earth. This was not possible due to the limited time available before they would be obliged to blast off on the return journey to Ganymede as well as to the limited number of spacesuits on the ship. They drew straws, and the three lucky winners donned their suits and stepped outside by means of the airlock.

What they found was sand, nothing but sand. It appeared to extend as far as they eye could see in all directions. Because the gravity of the earth was about seven times that on Ganymede, they found walking any length almost impossible. After covering a distance of a quarter of a mile and finding no signs of life, vegetable or animal, and nothing but sand, they decided they had to return to the ship. Back on board, they reported their disappointing findings to the others. There was no doubt. Earth contained no life. What had been mistakenly concluded to be such signs was obviously due to natural phenomena.

When the ship returned to Ganymede, the findings of the expedition were accepted. The most powerful telescopes were shifted away from observing Earth to Mars, where several scientists claimed they had detected canals. The defense firms, for their part, were extremely gratified with the results of the mission. Through clever lobbying, they obtained government funding for a program to construct a vehicle that a future expedition to Mars could use to explore the surface of the planet rather than having to do so on foot.

It is hard to know what fate would have had in store for either the inhabitants of Ganymede or the Earth of the mission had landed in another location. Fortunately or unfortunately, the spot where it set down was in the middle of the Sahara Desert.

Monkey Business

When Amos Hitherto, President of the Amalgamated Atheists' Society, resolved to disprove the existence of God scientifically, he threw all of his considerable energy into the project. Unhampered as he was by any feelings of religion, ethics, or morals, he had amassed a considerable fortune. This enabled him to allocate whatever funds were necessary.

Letherton's plan was to replicate the story he had heard about the lack of any divine involvement in the writing of Holy Scripture. He would do this by proving the assertion that a monkey, typing blindly in the cellar of the British Museum would, after many eons, type out a complete, perfect rendition of the King James Bible. Naturally, the choice of the right monkey was important. After considerable research into the subject, Letherton selected a young male chimpanzee named James who appeared to be unusually bright.

James was put at a desk, given a manual typewriter, and shown how to hit the keys with his fingers. There he was obliged to sit, typing away, for twelve hours a day, with only fifteen minutes off for lunch. When the animal rights group learned of this treatment and protested, Hitherto reluctantly agreed to permit James a fifteen minute break, even volunteering to furnish James, free of charge, a moderate sized banana at each break.

James's efforts produced tons and tons of foolscap covered

with gibberish. The floor of the room was eternally covered with discarded paper. Several times, Letherton thought he was on the brink of success. On one occasion, the researcher, who was supervising the project on a day to day basis, rushed to him with a triumphant cry, informing him that the monkey had typed a reasonably correct copy of an O'Henry short story. Convinced that he was on the right track and that James would soon produce the King James Bible, Letherton redoubled his efforts. As an inducement to speed James on, he increased the size of the bananas provided the chimpanzee.

The situation was repeated several years later, when James typed out a near perfect rendition of the first two acts of "Macbeth." This time, Letherton instructed his researcher to spur James on by lengthening his working day to thirteen hours. Years passed. James had obviously aged. He typed much more slowly, his hands, handicapped by rheumatism. Letherton too had aged. He now was obliged to spend many months a year away from the project, on vacation in Florida.

Then one day success came. The researcher, who had replaced his now retired predecessor, rushed into Letherton's office, crying ""Eureka!" James had finally succeeded. There on the desk next to him was a complete, perfectly typed manuscript of the King James Bible. Letherton was naturally, overjoyed. He had finally obtained the proof he desired, that the Bible was not written through the involvement of divine inspiration and that God perforce did not exist.

Letherton carefully made the arrangements for the announcement of his findings. He hired a large room at the National Press Club in the nation's capital and invited as many media representatives as he could. With the spotlight on him, he strode to the podium and announced that an ape had typed out the Bible and that this was irrefutable proof that God does not exist. Cameras clicked, and the news was spread throughout the world. Letherton settled back to reap the expected congratulations, possibly even the award of the Nobel Prize. Gratefully, he retired James to a farm in the country where he was provided with whatever delicacies he desired to eat.

Alas! The reaction was not what Letherton had expected. All the major religious groups interpreted the event as proving the existence of God. After all, they reasoned, only divine intervention could have led a chimpanzee to re-create the King James Bible. This conclusion was accepted by the media. Instead of closing, the various churches enjoyed a significant revival.

Letherton was crushed. He took to his bed, a broken man, and died a few months later. Ironically, his wife, who had never shared Letherton's atheistic views, prevailed upon him to be baptized and accepted into the Episcopal Church. He mumbled his acceptance wearily, and died a Christian. The moral of this story is inescapable. Letherton's experience neither proves nor disproves the existence of God, or of divine inspiration in the writing of the Bible. It does, however, provide irrefutable proof that you can spend vast sums of money without obtaining the ends you seek.

You Are What You Eat

The sign on the wall of the Quality Meat Market in Bayonne, New Jersey proclaimed in large letters "You Are What You Eat." It was put there to persuade prospective customers that it made sense to pay the higher prices charged by the butcher shop to purchase and eat the premium meats it sold. Bayonne was largely a working class town. Although the large navy base had terminated most of its operations since the end of the war, the majority of the men still worked at blue collar jobs in plants around Bayonne, many of them in the nearby petroleum refineries.

Jerry Sullivan had opened the shop when he returned from military service. With hard work and a little luck, the butcher shop thrived. Wages were good for the factory workers living in Bayonne, and they had the money to purchase the premium meats the Quality Meat Market sold. Jerry hired several workers to help him at the shop, and purchased a van to deliver meat to his customer's homes. He joined a local golf club and played golf every Wednesday afternoon; his wife Marry received a fur coat from him one Christmas and his son, Michael, was sent off to Notre Dame, the first member of the Sullivan family to go to College.

Over the years, however, the situation changed. Many of the factories around Bayonne closed their operations in New Jersey, moving their plants to lower wage states. Then the large supermarket chains moved into the area, selling meats at prices far lower than Jerry could afford. One after another, Jerry was forced to let his workers go, retaining only Paul McBride, who had served with him in the army, been wounded in the leg, and still walked with a pronounced limp.

Now business had fallen off so much, that Jerry knew he would soon have to close the butcher shop. As much as he hated to, he planned to give Paul his two weeks' notice that Saturday. Even after eliminating Paul's modest pay, he doubted that he would be able to send his son Michael back to Notre Dame for his senior year. And as for being able to send his daughter, Patricia Ellen, to college when she graduated from high school next year, that was too preposterous even to contemplate.

Jerry was seated at the back of the store, looking despondently at the wall clock. It was almost closing time, and there had been only two customers so far that day. He heard the bell signaling the entry of a customer, and turned to the door. A very tall, very slender man dressed entirely in black, his body enveloped in a black cape, had entered the shop. He wore a tall silk hat, of the kind Jerry had seen only in the old movies on TV, showing the upper classes at society parties.

"Good afternoon," said the visitor, speaking in a sepulchral voice. "Are you the proprietor of the Quality Meat Market?"

"I am," said Jerry. "What can I do for you?"

"My name is Underwood," said the visitor. "I am the representative in this area of the AAA Meat Service. We provide the highest quality meats to retailers, such as yourself, at the lowest possible price."

The last thing Jerry needed right then was more meat. "I'm sorry, Mr. Underwood," he said sadly. "I already have an excellent wholesaler. Please don't waste your time. I can't possibly buy any meat from you."

His words seemed lost on Underwood. From the folds of his cape, he extracted a sheaf of paper and laid it down in front of

Jerry. This is our price list. As you can see, the prices we charge are extremely competitive."

Jerry glanced at the sheet of paper. The prices charged were less than thirty percent of what he was currently paying. He knew there was no way in the world the AAA Meat Service could sell meat to him at that price. It had to be a scam.

Mr. Underwood," he said. "Your prices are good but I'm afraid my answer is still no."

Underwood was not the least perturbed. "Naturally," he said, "I appreciate your doubts. Allow me to explain the terms of our offer. We will provide you with the quantity of meat you sell each week entirely free of charge. It will give you the opportunity to try the meat, to see what your customers think of it and to sample it yourself. If at the end of the week you do not wish to give us further orders, we simply walk away with no charge to you. If, as we expect, you find our meat attaining or exceeding the quality of the meat you currently sell, you make us your regular supplier and purchase the meat at the prices shown in our price list.

Jerry stood silently, mulling over the offer. Try as he might, he was unable to find any catch. The way business was going, he certainly had to do something drastic. If the meat provided by Underwood was nearly as good as what he was now selling, one week's free supply would be a cash bonanza for him. He could keep Paul on a little longer. With a few additional economies, he might even be able to send his son back to college for his senior year.

"All right," he said slowly. "I accept your offer."

Underwood then explained the details of the delivery. Everything seemed routine except that Underwood insisted that the meat would have to be delivered at exactly midnight on Sunday. Try as he might, Underwood refused to budge. "Our delivery schedules," he said, "Are carefully coordinated, so that we can provide the meat at the price we charge. Any alteration would be far too costly. Reluctantly, Jerry had agreed.

There was one problem, Jerry had promised Mary that he

would go with her to an event at church on Sunday night. He arranged to have Paul be at the shop to handle the delivery at 12am. On Monday morning, he got to the store early, wondering if all had gone according to plan.

Paul arrived a few minutes later and assured him that all had gone well. The full order had been delivered by the AAA Meat Service. "They even added a few pounds of sausages we hadn't ordered," Paul reported. "The delivery man said that they had found it to be a popular item, and they think it will help increase our sales." Jerry inspected the meat. It seemed to be of excellent quality. Then he got an idea. With this week's supply of meat costing him nothing, he could reduce his prices to attract customers. He had Paul make up a large sign, which he placed in the window informing the public of "A ONE WEEK SPECIAL SALE ON ALL MEATS."

That night, Jerry took home one of the steaks that Underwood had supplied for dinner. Mary prepared it in the usual way, and he tasted it with apprehension. To his surprise, it was amazingly tender. The taste seemed slightly sweeter than usual, but he found himself savoring the meat. Patricia Ellen, who rarely ate much, surprised him by taking a large second helping. He cautiously told Mary that the steak tasted exceptionally good that night, but she took it as a compliment about her cooking ability.

During the rest of the week, the number of customers at the shop increased slightly, as passersby saw the sign and decided to give the store a try. He was particularly pleased by the comments from his steady customers, all of whom expressed pleasure at the improved quality of the steaks, roasts and chops they had purchased. When Mr. Underwood reappeared on Friday evening, Jerry happily wrote out a check for the next week's supply of meat and instructed him to add the Quality Meat Market to its list of regular customers.

Things at the store over the next couple of years proceeded on the same upward course. As sales rose, he was able to hire back first one, and then another of his former employees, and to give Paul a modest raise, the first he received in over five years. There was now no doubt about whether Michael would be able to finish college, and when he hesitantly mentioned he would like to go on to Law School, Jerry assured him it was an excellent idea, and that they could afford the tuition. Thanks to the very low price he was paying Underwood, he had reduced his prices to a level that forced the large supermarket chains to do the same. After a few months, they had closed their stores or shifted to types of meat that Jerry's shop did not sell.

Then, one Sunday, Paul called him to say he had come down with a bad cold, and that he wanted Jerry to handle the delivery at midnight of the week's meat supply. Jerry thought of asking one of his other clerks to fill in, but finally decided it would be less trouble to do it himself. Arriving at the shop a few minutes before midnight, Jerry settled down to await the delivery.

He did not have to wait long. Exactly at midnight, the bell signaling the door had been opened opened rang. Jerry looked up as a tall man, wearing a black wizard hat, entered the shop, carrying a large quarter of meat. It was not Mr. Underwood, but another man dressed in a black uniform. Jerry was surprised. He had expected to see Mr. Underwood. "Hello," he said, attempting to make conversation.

The man grunted something, then continued on to the back of the shop, putting the side of meat into the large store refrigerator. Jerry recalled with a start that Paul had not said anything about the meat deliveries for some time. It had become such a routine matter that Paul had not even mentioned it, and he had neglected to ask him about it. The man repeated his round trip between the door and the refrigerator, each time carrying a side of meat. He finished, then without further word, walked to the door.

Curious, Jerry followed him. As the door opened, Jerry watched him get into the meat delivery vehicle. He thought to himself that the driver was one of the most taciturn individuals he had ever seen. Then it struck him. The delivery truck looked exactly like a giant hearse. Jerry went home, his head swirling. He could not get what he had observed out of his mind. The next morning at breakfast, he was so silent that Mary asked what the matter was. He did not wish to alarm her, so he made up an excuse, kissed her goodbye, and drove off to the shop.

When Paul came in, he asked him if he had ever seen the delivery van. "Why yes," was his answer. "It looked just like a giant hearse."

Hearing someone else echo his own thoughts made it even worse. All the old questions came back. How could the AAA Meat Service sell him the meat so cheaply? Was the meat really beef, pork, and lamb, or from some other animal? What animal? Could it conceivably be human flesh? The possible answers were too horrible to contemplate.

What should he do? If he switched from the AAA Meat Service back to his old supplier, he would have to drastically raise his prices. It would be only a matter of time, probably no more than a few months before he would have to close the shop. He would have to lay off not just Paul, but also the other two clerks. Michael would have to drop out of Georgetown Law School, and Patricia Ellen would have to drop out of Trinity College. How could he cause such an upheaval, unless he were absolutely sure the meat was from legitimate sources?

It was too big a decision for Jerry to make on his own, so he cast about for someone he could consult. Mary was out of the question. He had never discussed the shop with her, and now she seemed totally preoccupied with her activities at the church. Both Michael and Patricia Ellen had good heads on their shoulders, but both were in Washington, DC at school. And even if they were home, it wasn't fair to discuss it with them at their age.

Next he thought of Father Mulhany, his priest. But the father, a saintly man, did not have the slightest bit of common sense. He would most likely tell Jerry to say the rosary, and ask God for guidance. Then the answer came to him. Monsignor Riley. His wife and the Riley children had all been childhood friends. They still remained close, playing golf occasionally at Jerry's club, and the Monsignor calling on Jerry's home most Christmas nights, to exchange Christmas greetings over a couple of drinks. He had excellent judgment and a wide range of experiences, having served for three years as a navy chaplain during the war. He was now in charge of a large, wealthy parish in the suburbs.

Obviously, he couldn't invite the Monsignor to dinner at his home and then raise the subject of the meat they had just eaten. That morning when Jerry got to the store, he telephoned the Monsignor. He was immediately connected and asked if he could come over and discuss a personal problem. The Monsignor apologized that he was tied up that evening, and suggested that Jerry come over the following day at whatever time was convenient for him.

The following day after closing the shop, Jerry had driven out to the Monsignor's church. He found the Monsignor in his office and, he greeted him warmly, suggesting that they might be more comfortable talking in his home. Leading Jerry next door into the living room of the rectory, the Monsignor poured him a generous drink, and took one for himself. When they had each seated themselves in a comfortable armchair, the Monsignor asked, "Is there a problem I can help you with, Jerry?

"Yes, there is," came the reply, and Jerry proceeded to tell the Monsignor the full story of his association with Mr. Underwood, the AAA Meat Service, and his rising concern over the source of the meat.

The churchman sat quietly for a few minutes thinking. He then stood, helped himself to another drink, and made the same for Jerry. "That is a difficult one," he said slowly.

There ensued a few more minutes of silence. Then the Monsignor spoke. "First of all," he said, "I am speaking to you now not as a priest, but as your friend. We clearly do not have enough information to reach a firm conclusion. If you terminate the meat contract, you will have to close your shop, fire your employees, and see your children drop out of school. You have no solid reasons, other than your unsubstantiated doubts, not to continue on with the contract, and it is unlikely that any immediate evil will occur. Your customers have been eating and enjoying the meat for several years, with no unfavorable consequences. I would, therefore, do nothing unless you get some firm proof of your suspicions.

Jerry expressed his gratitude to the Monsignor and drove home, much happier than before. He followed the Monsignor's advice, and all went well. However, he found he was enjoying the meat dinners at home far less than before, and asked Mary to serve fish at least four times a week in addition to the customary fish on Fridays. When she looked at him strangely, he explained that his cholesterol was creeping up, and he thought that the lesser consumption of meat would be better for him. He also noticed that when he invited the Monsignor for dinner at his home, his friend had either apologized pleading a prior engagement, or suggested that they eat at a restaurant instead.

Jerry kept the shop open until Patricia Ellen graduated from college. He offered to send her to law school, an interest she had expressed during her junior year, and had been surprised and slightly pleased when she told him she now wished to marry her old high school boy friend as soon as she graduated from college. Jerry promptly gave his employees a two month's advance notice of his plan to close the shop. He was worried about Paul's ability to get along, and was relieved when he made arrangements to live with his widowed sister, and share the costs.

Today Jerry and Mary are comfortably retired, living in a retirement community next to a golf course in Florida. Mary is amazed at his improved health, and the fact that he can now eat meat for dinner every day but Friday. The couple remain close to their children, who still reside in New Jersey, but visit them regularly several times a year. Jerry enjoys playing with his grandchildren and is teaching the oldest boy how to play golf. On the days when he isn't playing golf, Jerry goes to the local library, where he has taught himself to use a computer.

One day at the library, he was tempted to use his new computer proficiency to look up the bona fides of the AAA Meat Service. However, he decided against it. He told himself, "What you don't know can't hurt you."

Rocks

Professor Throckmorton's announcement of his discovery that rocks can reason and can communicate with each other was met with widespread skepticism and ridicule. The general consensus was that Throckmorton has regrettably suffered a nervous breakdown or as one late night TV humor show quipped, "Throckmorton has rocks in his head."

Throckmorton tried to convince the scientific authorities of the validity of his claims, but this was hard to do. The problem was that rocks communicate in a frequency so low that it cannot be detected by most instruments, to say nothing of the human ear. Again, it turned out that rocks are by nature taciturn, and rarely speak and only when they have something of significance to say.

Although a brilliant researcher, the professor had come upon his discovery purely by chance. He had been conducting research into the phenomena that precede earthquakes in the hope of finding a more accurate method of predicting their timing and strength. To his surprise, his sensitive instruments had picked up what appeared to be verb communication between rocks alerting each other to the approaching geological disturbance.

Throckmorton was fully cognizant of the immense potential of his discovery. If communication with rocks could be established, humans could obtain not only advance warning of earthquakes, but also of volcanic eruptions and tidal waves. The commercial opportunities were equally significant. Geological surveys to find petroleum and mineral deposits would be greatly facilitated. Even archeologists would benefit from learning the location of artifacts long buried under the soil.

After several years, Throckmorton's limited financial resources were exhausted, and he sought funding from his university's physics department. Strife and personal rivalries were high among his colleagues and his request was rejected unanimously by his colleagues. They went so far as to suggest that if he were not a tenured professor, he would have been immediately fired for making such a proposal. One even raised the possibility of declaring Throckmorton insane and discharging him on those grounds, his tenured status notwithstanding.

Professor Throckmorton was not a man to be easily rebuffed. He appealed over their heads to the university president. A well know politician who had lost his last race and considering his university post a stepping stone to higher political office. The president rudely interrupted the professor's presentation and threw him out of the office. A proposal to the National Science Foundation fared no better. Throckmorton's written proposal was answered by a one sentence form letter.

A lesser man would have been defeated, but not Throckmorton. He carefully a drafted a new proposal for funding and sent it off to the National Science Foundation. This time, the professor omitted any reference to rock's being rational or to their ability to communicate. His proposal stated that the purpose of his proposed research was to study the agricultural potential of the soils of sub-Saharan Africa with a view to combating malnutrition among the indigenous populations. Acting quickly for a government office, the National Science Foundation approved the full sum Throckmorton had requested. So great was his glee, that the professor's conscience troubled him not at all, since no one could reasonably argue that rocks are not part of the sib-Saharan soil.

When his grant ran out, Throckmorton easily secured from the National Science Foundation a continuation of the project. From time to time he had modest success. On one occasion he communicated a small piece of quartz, but found it flighty and unwilling or unable to discuss the matters Throckmorton brought up. On another occasion he learned from a rock on the New Jersey seacoast that there was a deposit of silver nearby, only to be disappointed after excavation at the specified point uncovered only a silver dollar buried in the sand.

As the years passed, Throckmorton spent increasingly less energy in pursuing the rock research. As memories faded about his sensational announcement, he was accorded greater respect. No criticism was raised when he was selected to head the Physics Department and there is talk he will be named the next dean of the College of Science.

The professor has shed most of his teaching duties and spends the bulk of his time presiding over the large new research laboratory that was created especially for him to investigate the problems of hunger in Africa. The funding has been most generous thanks to the influential member of Congress in whose district the laboratory was established. This Congressman cares not a whit for Africa or hunger but is pleased with the many jobs he expects it will create for his constituents.

Throckmorton very much enjoys his lunch each day prepared by the gourmet chef who runs the kitchen at the laboratory's dining facility. This amenity is due to the general language contained in the legislation authorizing the financing of the laboratory, which provides that some of the funds may be utilized to provide appropriate eating facilities for the staff.

The professor's conscience occasionally troubles him as when he heard of the latest large California earthquake. He is well aware that if he had convinced the scientific community about the validity of his findings, some lives and much property damage could have been avoided. He handles his regrets by reminding himself

that scientific truth is not what it really is but about what a majority of scientists think it is and that he therefore bears no personal
responsibility for what is occurring.

Putin For President

The Putin for President Movement seemed at first glance totally Quixotic. Not only was the Russian President widely regarded in the United States as opposed to everything this country stood for, but he had been born in Russia and was thus barred under the Constitution from serving as president. Nonetheless, as the time for the 2016 presidential election approached, it was obvious that the majority of the supporters of both major parties were so dissatisfied with all of the leading candidates that they would probably refuse to vote. Political pollsters admitted openly that their polls were useless in predicting the outcome of the race because so few potential voters would voice any opinion on the candidates other than to utter unrepeatable vulgarities.

The first public call for President Putin to be nominated as President of the United States appeared on the editorial page of the "New York Times" in the form of a letter to the editor. It was obviously not considered to be a series proposal; the paper's editorial staff labeling it "A Touch of Political Humor." One curious element of the story is that when an investigative reporter sometime later checked the purported name and address of the letter's author, he determined it belonged to a fence-painter who had died two years before the date the letter was said to be written.

The letter would probably have passed unnoticed expect for

the fact that it was seen by an editor of CBS News, who suggested it be used in a humorous signing off piece for the network's nightly TV news show. When his proposal was accepted, and the letter aired, the cat was out of the bag. Because of the tendency of all of the prime time network news shows to use the next day any item carried by a rival network that they had omitted, follow-up stories were carried by the ABC, NBC and Fox Network news shows on the following day. As I usual, CNN then ventured the fray, putting on a three-hour evening special on the subject of Putin for President equipped with the leading political "talking heads" and two former American presidents

Once the possibility of Putin being elected President of the United States became a topic of public conversation, popular support for the idea mounted. From a tiny trickle, it grew into a brook, then a mighty river. Soon it became an unstoppable tidal wave.

The Russian President helped his own cause by his astute political behavior. When first asked about the possibility by journalists, he gave the standard answer demanded by politician's tradition in such circumstances. He stated that he had no plans beyond carrying out his functions as Russian President for his elected term in office. Sometime later, as his political base in the United States grew, he admitted that he would be willing to serve as American President if drafted by a convention and elected by the voters.

Simultaneously Putin exploited the American media, freely making himself available to the Sunday morning TV network news shows. On "Face the Nation," he was pressed hard by the host to explain his role in the Russian invasion of Ukraine. His response, "As President of a nation I would deem it my duty to protect and defend the interests of that national above all others," was widely applauded by Americans of all political parties, eager to see the administration in Washington that would actually consider American interests first.

His answer to a question on "Meet the Press" as to whether as American President he would commit U.S. ground forces to combat in the Middle East was similarly well received. Putin declared that the president of any country has a solemn obligation never to put a single member of his country's armed forces at risk unless the vital interests of that nation were at stake. When interviews asked Putin to state his position on the thorny issues of gun control and abortion, the Russian President appreciated the danger. However he came down on the issue he would alienate voters on the other side. Accordingly he answered in Russian rather than in English and spoke so rapidly that no translator could possibly understand what he had said. Asked to repeat his answer, he did so in the same manner.

Attention now turned to the inability of the Russian President, even if nominated and elected, to serve as President because of the Constitutional requirement that this post be filled only by a "natural born" citizen of the United States. As interest in Putin's possible candidacy grew, attention turned to amending the Constitution to permit this. Congress was so bitterly divided that no significant legislation had been passed by both houses in several years. Therefore, the lead was taken by the various state legislatures using a method provided for in the Constitution, but never before attempted.

The legislature of the state of Arizona, furious about the administration's policy on immigration and border control, took the lead. It passed a resolution calling for the holding of a national convention to propose new amendments to the Constitution of the United States. Other states rushed to follow suit, and the required two-thirds total was quickly surpassed. The National Convention met in Chicago and seriously considered only one new amendment. As passed, this stated that "In addition to any native born citizen of the United States, an individual who has served two consecutive four-year terms as an elected president of a country holding a permanent seat on the United Nations Security council shall be eligible to be elected and to serve as President of the United States."

After its passage by the National Assembly, the proposed amendment went to the states for ratification. State legislatures vied with each other to have the honor of being the first to ratify. Maine, New York, Mississippi California and Hawaii all ratified it on the same day, with California and Hawaii alleging that they were unfairly treated because they were in Western time zones. Within a few months the required three-fourths of the states had ratified the new Twenty-Eighth Amendment, and it became a fundamental part of the American Constitution. The so-called "Putin Amendment," was the first new amendment to be added since the Twenty-Seventh in 1992, which prevented Congress from increasing its own pay until after a new session begins..

Unfortunately, ratification was completed before the Iowa Caucuses and the deadline for entering the New Hampshire primaries had passed. In Iowa, a plurality of delegates selected at the caucuses were individuals who pledged that if Putin ran, they would give him their support. In Iowa, Putin won both the Republic and Democratic Presidential primaries because of a landslide of write-in votes. His victories in every succeeding state primary led the Republican National Convention in August and the Democratic National Convention in September to each nominate Putin for President of the United States by acclamation. For his running mate, Putin surprised the public by announcing that Russian Prime Minister Dmitry Medvedev would join him on the ticket. To a few timid objections that Medvedev was barred from the ticket because of his Russian birth, Putin answered that whatever technical problems that might exist were very minor in nature and would be handled by him administratively.

With Putin running against himself as the candidate of both the Republican and Democratic Parties, the result was a foregone conclusion. The final electoral vote was almost evenly split, with Putin winning a slightly larger number of votes in the Electoral College as the Republican candidate than he did as the Democratic Candidate. As the date for Putin's inauguration as the forty-fifth

President of the United States, his support among all sectors of the public is the highest any new American President has ever enjoyed. The Defense Industry views him as a President who will, favor powerful and well-equipped armed forces and will support greatly increased American spending on defense. All elements of the business community are confident he will favor healthy profits by firms as long as they support his governmental policies and contribute to any projects he regards as important. The general public knows that under President Putin, opposition in Washington to proposals urged by the administration will unfailingly pass both houses of Congress. In short, America is looking forward to a period of peace and harmony in both the domestic and foreign arenas unknown in our history.

Erskine's Law

You may search where you will in any reference book and any library in the world for some mention of John Erskine or of Erskine's Law. You will be unsuccessful. That is because John FitzJames Erskine and Erskine's Law have been deliberately excised from human history. In effect, he now has never existed. He is buried in an unmarked grave. His birth certificate, death certificate, all government records relating to him have been destroyed or permanently misplaced.

Erskine's early life was perfectly normal. Born in a small Ohio city the only child of two parents who were school teachers, he received good grades in high school. Recognizing his potential, his parents managed to scrape together enough money to permit him to attend the local state university. There, he did so well majoring in economics that his professors arranged for him to receive a scholarship to pursue graduate studies at the University of Chicago, and then regarded as one of the leading centers for advanced economic research.

Receiving his doctoral degree, Erskine taught as an instructor at Michigan State for two years, then took a high-paying job at the prestigious Brooking Institution in Washington, D.C. It is there that he began the research that was to lead to his discovery of Erskine's Law. When he found he missed teaching classes and the personal contact with students, he moved on to Harvard University, where he was named to a titled professorship.

It was at Harvard that he completed his research and published his law in a small scholarly journal. A shy man, he was not seeking publicity, but rather hoped to arouse comment and criticism of his law from other economics professors. In his heart, he was appalled by the possible implications of his law had hoped that one of his contemporaries would be able to find flaws in it.

In simple English, the law states that wealth is neither created nor destroyed. It thus might be considered a corollary of the law that matter cannot either be created or destroyed and no more likely to cause significant discord and controversy than the latter. For several months, Erskine's article passed unnoticed. Then a professor at Stanford University published a critique of Erskine's Law.

.The criticism asserted that both the Industrial Revolution and the invention of the computer ushered in periods of rapid economic growth in which tremendous wealth was created. Given the opportunity to reply, Professor Erskine answered that, in fact, the apparent increase in wealth linked to those events actually represented a borrowing of wealth potential that had been untapped for centuries and was now being spent. The cost of this wealth represented a transfer of wealth to the generations benefitting from it from the future generations which would no longer have it available.

Recognizing that his explanation would not be accepted by many, Erskine included in his response details of the mathematical formulas he had devised to support it. News of the academic debate spread and stories about it began to appear in the popular media. Erskine's formulas were carefully analyzed and subjected to the most detailed computer analysis. The conclusions were horrifying. Erskine was correct! All of the beliefs and the programs stemming from them over the ages were not just flawed but totally wrong and useless.

Once the ramifications of Erskine's Law were recognized, there was widespread panic in government circles and the board rooms of corporations. The procedures and policies that had served as a guideline for society would have to be abandoned. Aid to the less advantaged, according to Erskine's calculations, would not benefit society as a whole, merely represent a shift in wealth from those who had to those who did not. While this simple fact should have been readily apparent, it was normally disguised from public view. Now it became totally clear. So, too, were other government programs, such as Social Security and Medicare.

Similar recalculations occurred in the commercial sector. Wages increases obviously represented a shift in wealth from stockholders to investors, management salaries and stock options a shift in wealth from both labor and investors to management. The confusion, chaos and discord rose to such a high level that the civilization was itself in peril. There was only one logical solution. Erskine and his law must no longer exist.

The timely death of Professor Erskine almost immediately followed. He had been traveling on a regularly-scheduled commercial jet from Boston to a speaking engagement at the University of Chicago. The brief report of the incident appeared on in the back pages of the few newspapers that carried it. The story reported that when the plane encountered strong turbulence, one of the cabin doors had been forced open. In the disturbance caused in the passenger compartment one unlucky passenger, Professor Erskine, had been yanked out of his seat and been projected out the door, despite the frantic efforts by a cabinet attendant to save him.

At about the same time Professor Anne Howard, Erskine's fiancée and a brilliant economist in her own right, suffered a nervous breakdown in which she suffered the delusion that she had known, studied under and then become engaged to a fictional colleague named John Erskine. This delusion defied all psychiatric attempts to cure her, resulting in her permanent confinement in the luxurious psychiatric institution used only by the nations rich and famous. She was allowed to pursue her academic research and furnished whatever she wished, all at government expense.

As Erskine's parents were dead and he had no other living relatives to mourne him, his existence effectively perished from human ken. New issues of the economics journal which had published Erskine's Law and the subsequent commentary on it were furnished all libraries that had copies of them in their collections, and the originals destroyed. The archives of Harvard University, the Brookings Institution, the University of Chicago and Ohio State were all similarly corrected to eliminate and mention of Erskine. Not even the yearbooks from his high school escaped the purging.

Since Erskine and his law had never existed, it was an easy matter for government and industry revert to their traditional practices. Welfare, Social Security, Medicare, stock options and wage increases were no more disputed than before. If Professor Erskine had been a real person, a wise observer might have learned one thing from this event. When truth becomes too uncomfortable to accept, the wisest course is to simply ignore it.

SNAFU

As Joshua Oates scrutinized the data from the giant super computer, he realized there could be no possible doubt. Everything in the world that could go wrong was going wrong. The weather was worsening year after year at an accelerating rate. Colder winters combined with warmer summers; the polar icecaps were melting, seismic activity and volcanic eruptions, from supposedly long extinct volcanoes, were causing not only property damage, but more often also loss of life. The life expectancy rates in the advanced nations were climbing, at the same time as the birth rate in the less developed nations soared, producing growing populations that could not be fed. Unemployment rates climbed; wages fell. In the Mid-West, mutant giant man-eating ants had emerged from the corn fields and forced the evacuation of all the inhabitants of Des Moines and several smaller towns.

Oates was a conscientious scientist and read and reread the computer readout repeatedly. Each time, it was the same. He instructed the technicians to take the computer apart, and examine every component for a failed part. Then they reassembled the computer, and Oates ran through the data readout. The result was the same. Oates knew it was his responsibility to alert his superiors of the awful news. This, however, was not a simple matter.

The giant super computer furnishing the data was the keystone of a top secret project by the NSA to collect, collate, and analyze all of the data in the world. The purpose was to provide policy options to the American President. The project was so highly classified that its existence or findings could never be disclosed. This obviously was a serious obstacle in the way of Oates' informing anyone of his disturbing findings. Finally, after considerable thought, he put them down in a memo that he gave the highest possible security classification. Only one copy was made, and this was delivered by an armed courier, personally into the hands of the President's Adviser for National Security Affairs.

The Adviser took one look at the memo and was appalled. He realized that if word of the contents were ever linked to anyone, it would be clear that all of the administration's policies, past, present, and future, were totally useless. He immediately burned the memo, and flushed the ashes down the toilet. As a precaution, he then destroyed his computer hard drive and issued instructions in the President's name for Oates to be immediately escorted out of his office by armed guards, prevented from speaking to anyone, or taking anything with him, and was to be flown in a sealed plane to a distant island off Guam. There, in almost complete isolation, he was, to take up his new post as supervisor of the computer project dealing with Pacific fish movements. Needless to say, all of Oates' files were destroyed without being read.

Because the National Security Adviser neglected to order that the project be terminated, it continued, with one of Oates' subordinates taking charge. He had just seated himself at the console of the giant super computer when the readout abruptly changed. Instead of producing data, the readout kept repeating over and over again the phrase "situation hopeless; a further compilation of data futile." As the man at the console stared in awe, and the technicians assisting him dumbly watched, the computer gave itself the command to self-destruct. It began emitting clouds of acrid black smoke and then exploded, showering the room with debris and severely injuring many of those in the room.

The destruction of the super computer was followed swiftly by the collapse of human civilization around the world. Power systems failed; transportation networks crumbled. Produce lay rotting in the fields while urban populations starved. The earth's population was literally decimated, and then decimated again. One of the last survivors was Oates, who lived on comfortably for some time on his remote Pacific isle, subsisting on the fish specimens that had been collected as part of his project.

With the demise of the human race, other species vied viciously to become the dominant life form on the planet. The competition was finally won by the genus rattus, known commonly as the rat. Key factors in the rat's victory were its high level of intelligence, small size, which enabled it to subsist on a minimum of food and its ability to eat a wide variety of food stuffs. Those few humans who exist today, do so as house pets in rat households, where they are usually well treated. There are occasionally unconfirmed reports about isolated humans surviving in the wild, most often in the jungles of New Guinea.

The Cat's Meow

Hope Treason had reached the age of forty-three still a spinster, despite the many amorous escapades she had engaged in as a young woman. Unfortunately, none of the men she had met had satisfied the high levels she had in her mind. They all lacked the necessary level of intelligence, sense of humor, pleasant personality and solid financial footing. As a result, she was now living alone in her little town house in the prestigious northwest part of our nation's capital known as Georgetown, with her pet cat Rasputin as her only live-in companion. She had no close friends other than several of her ex-beaux, whose occasional companionship she continued to enjoy, even as they dated or married women with lower standards than Hopes'.

Hope held a senior, rather well paid position in the administrative side of the State Department. This was not related at all to her extensive knowledge of international affairs or to her having earned a Ph.D. degree in Russian history from one of the Ivy League universities. Both her parents held professorial posts in international relations, and from early childhood she had wanted to follow in their footsteps.

Her graduation from the university had unfortunately coincided with one of the temporary economic slumps that afflict the American economy, so that university teaching positions that year were difficult to obtain. As the weeks of unemployment turned into months, she began applying for virtually any job that seemed appropriate. When she went for a personal interview which was part of the State Department procedures for job applicants, she had absolutely no expectation of being hired. Her appearance at the interview was solely aimed at honing her performance for potential future interviews.

Much to her surprise, Hope had been hired for the post. She now headed a unit of the Department providing technical support to one of the Department's Bureaus. Her unit comprised some twenty-two employees of various grades, organized into four sections.

Hope found the work both extremely boring and frustrating. She had little interest in the technical matters which she now had to supervise. Even worse, all of her staff was of very low competence, with no interest in improving their performance. They had been hired as a result of pressure on their behalf from influential members of Congress or from powerful political donors and regarded their jobs as sinecures

The low level of their performance was not in itself particularly important. Very little of the work demanded of her unit actually was necessary, mostly consisting of periodic reports on inventory levels that were never read by their recipients. Hope, however, was acutely aware of her employees' failure to perform the requests laid down and so did them all herself, usually after one or more of her staff had turned in unacceptable responses.

One Tuesday morning, after some three and a half frustrating years on the job, Hope was seated at her desk laboring away when she realized she had left at home a report she had been drafting there the previous evening. As it was almost lunch time, she got up, left her office and went down to her car in the State Department garage. She was senior enough to enjoy a reserved parking space, so she envisioned no problem in driving to her nearby house in Georgetown, retrieving the draft report, and returning to her office within the sixty minutes officially allotted for lunch. Hope did not take this step lightly. The State Department Executive Dining Room, to which Hope was granted access because of her rank, usually served stewed apples on Tuesdays, and it was a dish she especially enjoyed.

The traffic that day was unusually heavy, and she was then obliged to park several blocks away from her house because the parking spaces along her street were occupied. By the time she reached her home, she was feeling sorry she had started on the trip. Climbing the front steps, Hope unlocked the door and stepped in. To her amazement she heard someone speaking. It was obviously coming from the second floor, from the smaller of the two bedrooms which she had turned into an office.

Hope was frightened. Someone must have broken in. She had no weapon in her house, but armed herself with a large kitchen knife and quietly crept upstairs. She peaked into the small bedroom and was shocked by what she saw and heard. Her pet cat, Rasputin was seated at her desk speaking into what appeared to be a small transmitter.

"This is Xilback Four calling Xilback Controller" she heard him say, "Come in, please. This is an emergency message. Come in, please. My ship has crashed on earth and cannot be repaired. Request immediate retrieval." Rasputin kept repeating these words, apparently receiving no response.

Hope stood there silently for a minute, then silently crept back downstairs and tiptoed out of the house. Sitting in her car, she found she still had the kitchen knife with her. She placed it on the front seat, looked at her watch, and realized she had to rush to get back to her office on time.

Back at her desk, Hope found it impossible to work. She could not get out of her mind the image of Rasputin speaking that strange message repeatedly into a transmitter. Had she really seen it, or had it been a dream?

This was no small matter to Hope. She loved Rasputin. She had grown up in a house with a cat, her parents favoring them as pets. When she had left her family home and moved to Washington to work at the State Department, she had thought about acquiring a pet cat for herself. Only concern that she might not be able to provide adequate care for a pet if she went away to the beach during the summer weekends had dissuaded her.

Actually, it is not as though Hope adopted Rasputin. Rather, the cat had adopted her. Their meeting occurred one morning, about six months after Hope had moved in. She was rushing on her way to the State Department, opened her front door, and was amazed to see the top step occupied by a sorry looking black and orange striped cat. It looked the worse for wear much. Its fur was dirty and in clumps, a scab covering a sore on its back. Hope had a tender heart, and she had been conditioned by her parents to treat house cats very much like unfortunate people.

As might have been predicted, she scooped the animal up in her arms, carried it to her kitchen, and attempted to clean it up, using warm water and a paper towel. The cat surprisingly submitted to her ministrations and even purred. It was getting quite late, so Hope gave the cat a saucer of milk, left it drinking happily and rushed off to the State Department.

Hope had one of her frequently frustrating days at the office and returned home exhausted. Her only thought was to kick off her shoes, take a hot bath and go to bed. Going upstairs to her bedroom, she was amazed to see the cat curled up, sleeping happily on her bed. While she had been gone, the cat had somehow managed to clean itself up. The orange and black fur looked quite clean, and the sore on its back had disappeared.

The cat awakened, lifted its head and stared at her. It looked much like any other stray cat one might glimpse on the street except for one thing; its eyes were a brilliant green, with flecks of gold. It purred, stood up, and Hope realized that although it was no longer than the average domestic cat, it was surprisingly slender and stood some fifty percent taller.

"I wonder what species it is?" she asked herself. "It's quite an unusual one. I will have to look it up."

Hope saw further than the cat was obviously a male. This posed the question of what she should call him. All of the cat names she had carried in her mind were for female cats.

"What about George?" she asked him. "Do you like it?" The cat made no response. He exhibited a similar indifference to "Harry" and "Dexter." Possibly he preferred more traditional CAT NAMES. "Is 'Boots' and better? Or 'Whiskers'?"

Still no response. After some minutes, during which the cat stared at her, she thought about less common names he might prefer. Because of her studies in East European history, it was natural that her mind turned to that area for possible cat names. "Stalin" or "Lenin" might cause her problems with State Department Security. Then she had a brilliant idea. "How do you like 'Rasputin?' she asked.

The cat meowed. His bright green eyes bore into hers. He seemed to blink one eye roguishly. "All right," she said, "Rasputin it is."

And so it was. Rasputin quickly became her best friend. No matter how tired she was from the office, each day when she arrived home she felt happy about the warm welcome she would receive from the cat. Sometimes, he would be sleeping quietly on her bed. More often, she would see him standing on the desk in her upstairs bedroom, peering through the window, looking for to get out of her car and come into the house.

Almost always, Rasputin would be waiting for her on the floor. As soon as she approached, he would leap up in one bound, grab her around the neck with his two front paws, and hug her warmly. Accompanying the leap would be a loud purring from the cat, which would last several minutes. Even if she attempted to put him on to the floor and feed him, he would resist until he obtained what he regarded as the proper amount of affection.

In the face of such heart-felt love and admiration, Hope began to spend most evenings at home with the cat, both of them sitting on the living room sofa, sharing a warm blanket, and watching television. Rufus would watch most programs with some interest, but surprisingly gave the greatest attention to network news shows.

Now, this feeling of comradeship with the cat seemed to be threatened. What she had seen indicated that Rasputin was not an ordinary cat, most probably not a cat at all. Cats, as far as is known, do not converse in English or speak into transmitters. How could she be friendly with that, whatever that was?

Returning from her office that night, Hope's usual feeling of joyous expectation over the warm welcome from Rasputin was missing. She did not see him peering out from the bedroom window. Climbing the stair to her bedroom, she felt a sense of dread over what she might encounter. She entered the bedroom and, to her relief, found Rasputin curled up on her bed comfortably sleeping.

The cat opened his eyes, stared at her for a moment, then jumped off the bed and raced to her feet. Then he leaped straight up, grabbed her around the neck, and began purring loudly. How could she resist? She hugged him. In response, he nestled his nose in her cheek and began licking her with his tongue.

Clearly, Hope thought, she had imagined that bizarre scene that afternoon. Cats certainly do not speak English, certainly do not use transmitters. She fed him as usual and that night, the two of them enjoyed watching news programs on TV, curled up on the sofa and sharing the same blanket.

The next morning, Hope went off to the office and life at home resumed its normal course. Hope thought no more of what she now regarded as a fantasy until the day her credit card bill arrived. Before paying it, she always examined the items closely, insuring that nothing had been mistakenly charged to her account.

One source of billings that was always there was for the home delivery of pizzas. It was a dish she very much enjoyed, although to avoid undue consumption of junk food, Hope usually rationed herself to just one home delivery a week. Very often, she would find herself billed for five or six deliveries a month, but Hope ascribed the discrepancy to poor memory on her part.

This month, the bill listed six home deliveries. As she sat at her office desk, trying to recall exactly how many times she had had pizza last month, her eyes came across an entry which startled her, a $1,264 charge for a book from a London antique book dealer. This had to be a mistake. The book was entitled "Egyptian Scientific Monographs, Volume II." Hope had not the least interest in Egyptian Scientific Monographs and had certainly not ordered it from the London dealer.

Out of curiosity, Hope looked up the book dealer on her computer. She not only found the dealer listed, but also a brief description of the book. It was published in 1808, with volume II devoted almost entirely to a discussion of an Eleventh Century manuscript on ancient Egyptian science. A footnote asserted that there were only three known copies of the work believed to be in existence and that the item in question was no longer available for purchase.

Hope straightaway called her credit card company and informed them that she had definitely not purchased the book and would deduct the $1,264 from the payment she was sending them. So good was her credit standing, that the credit card company had no wish to lose her as a customer. The charge for the book was removed from her account; Hope did not know or care how the obvious miss-billing had occurred.

A month or so later, Hope was at the office when she suddenly remembered it was her father's birthday on that Friday. Whenever it was possible, she had always tried to be home with her parents to help celebrate their respective birthdays. This year, the press of business at the office would not permit her to visit home, but she had purchased a large umbrella as a birthday present for her father, since he loved to walk and frequently came home soaked from being caught out on a walk by a rainstorm. The umbrella, extremely light and easy to carry, would be something he could use to keep himself from getting drenched in a downpour.

Hope wanted very much to have the umbrella reach her father by his birthday. The only solution was to drive home, pick up the umbrella, which had already been wrapped, and mail the package at the post office on her way back to the office. Taking an early lunch, she went down to the State Department garage, got into her car and drove home.

Hope entered her house; her thoughts concentrated on locating the umbrella and getting it to the post office to mail within the time left of her lunch hour, Suddenly, she became aware of a voice emanating from her office upstairs. Softly she climbed the stairs, taking pains to make no noise. There was no mistake. The refrain was familiar: "This is Xilback Four calling Xilback Controller. Come in Please. This is an emergency message. My ship has crashed on earth and cannot be repaired. Request immediate retrieval."

Peeking into the room, Hope confirmed what she suspected. There could be no possible mistake. Rasputin was seated at her desk, repeating the phrase over and over again. She did not know what to do. What to say? Should she confront him or pass it off as a big joke? Uncertain as to the proper response, she retreated downstairs as silently as she had mounted the stairs, left the house, returned to her car, and drove back to the State Department.

Needless to say, she was unable to do any work. As soon as the wall clock indicated the formal end of the business day, she left her office and drove home. Her house, when she entered it, seemed perfectly normal. She climbed the stairs and entered her bedroom. Rasputin was sleeping quietly on her bed. Everything appeared perfectly normal. It would be so easy to close her mind to what she had witnessed only a few hours before.

As she stood there, deep in thought, Rasputin opened his eyes, jumped off the bed and raced to her feet and leaped up, grabbing her neck with his paws as he had done so many nights before. He began to purr and to lick her face. This time, Hope's reaction was

different. Grabbing him roughly, she pushed him hard down onto
the bed. The cat looked at her with his brilliant green eyes, and his
purring trailed off. They stared at each other silently.

"All right," she said her voice cold and steely, "Do you have
something you wish to tell me?"

The cat didn't answer. Hope rarely lost her temper, but it was a
mistake to rile her. On those few occasions it occurred, the recipients of her wrath learned how ruthless she could be.

"Rasputin or whatever your name is. I know you can understand every word I say and that you speak perfect English. I came
home at lunch time and heard you talking into your transmitter.
Should I address you as 'Xilback Four?'" she added sarcastically.

The cat's green eyes peered into hers. Then he said, "I'm glad I
no longer have to play this charade. I really didn't enjoy deceiving
you. I have come to regard you as a close friend, and I am certainly
grateful for your taking me into your home. Xilback Four," he added, "Is not my name but my call signal to Xilback Control. My real
name would be far too difficult for you to pronounce. I come from
a planet at the far side of the Galaxy and from a civilization far in
advance of that on earth."

"All right," Hope said, and then paused. It was hard to believe
what the cat was saying. Still, if it was true, it would explain what
she had seen and heard. "What do I call you?" she asked.

"Please continue to call me Rasputin. I like the name. I have
studied your history and culture, and I know all about the Russian
peasant mystic Rasputin and his strong political influence in the
court of the last Russian Tsar, Nicolas II."

Hope pondered these words. "Then please tell me what you
are doing her?" she asked skeptically.

"As you probably heard me tell Xilback Control," the cat answered, "That my ship crashed on earth. Earth is the section of the
Galaxy I am responsible for, and I have to visit the area frequently
to make certain things are not getting out of hand. Those nuclear
explosions you have been conducting have alarmed my people.

Unfortunately, my ship's propulsion system failed and I was unable to land the craft properly. When I determined it was too badly damaged for me to repair, I was obliged to destroy it."

"Why destroy it?" Hope inquired.

"Come now," Rasputin answered. You're intelligent enough to have figured out the reason. We certainly don't want earthlings to study the space craft and possible construct one. Not with your low levels of intelligence and propensity to experiment with dangerous weapons. Fortunately," the cat went on, "I had been thoroughly briefed on what I should do if my space ship crashed here. I also took off all my clothing and destroyed the garments at the same time."

"Why go around without clothes?" Hope asked, puzzled. "Of course, your fur is attractive, but I would think that after wearing clothing, you'd be embarrassed walking around Washington naked."

It does take some time to get used to," the cat admitted. But I couldn't take the risk of being identified as an extraterrestrial. If my true nature were to become known, I would either be encaged in a laboratory and studied and possibly be dissected by your scientists or lynched by religious fanatics claiming I could not be intelligent because I am not made in the image of your God. Fortunately, I look enough like one of your domestic cats to be able to pass as one."

Hope could not argue with the cat's logic. "Well then," she asked, "How did you end up on my front step?"

"That's simple," he responded. "The telepathic powers of my species are rather limited, certainly when compared to some of the other intelligent species in the Galaxy. However, they were sufficient for me to observe while passing your house that some individual living there liked cats and was hoping to adopt one. The solution to my dilemma was there before me. I lay down on your step to wait until you opened the door and found me. It was a virtual certainty that you would take me in and make me comfortable.

To increase my chances of success, I messed up my fur to appear forlorn, even putting an imitation scab on my back."

Hope sat back and thought over all that Rasputin had said. She could, of course, simply throw him out, but that didn't seem charitable. Moreover, he had become a friend. Now that she could speak with him, he would be an even better companion. "All right," she said. "What do you propose we do?"

"I can appreciate your reluctance," the cat said softly, "And if you wish me to leave, I will do so quietly. However, I would very much like to stay with you. I have no earth coins to pay for the added cost, but I will try to make myself even more useful to you than I was in the past."

"Useful?" she asked dubiously.

"You know the sump pump you have in the basemen?" he explained. "Remember you found one day that there was water in the basement, and the pump didn't work. You planned to call a repairman when you returned home from work. I repaired it while you were away, and led you downstairs to the basement when you returned home. It was difficult persuading you to follow me, and I couldn't speak to you without revealing I was not really an earth cat."

"So that's why the sump pump worked that evening," Hope said. "I wondered how it had somehow repaired itself." She found herself automatically petting Rasputin and stopped, abruptly. To cover her embarrassment she asked, "Were you responsible for the extra pizzas I was charged for on my credit card bill?"

"I was," he said, looking ashamed and hanging his head. "It was easy for me as I knew your credit card number. I tried to limit my orders and hoped you wouldn't notice them."

"But why?"

"It's that dry cat food you've been feeding me. It's edible but no more than that. How would you like to eat that stuff and nothing else? I used to watch you eating the pizza each week with my mouth watering, but I couldn't ask you for a piece."

Hope had to admit Rasputin's justification was reasonable. "All right," she said. "From now on, when I order a pizza I will share it with you."

"But what about that rare Egyptian book I was charged for? Were you somehow involved in that? What on earth would you want with an antique book on that subject?"

Rasputin looked more ashamed. "It was a rare case of an error in judgment on my part. I browse the internet daily using your computer while you're at the office. When I came across that ad by the London dealer, I was curious about the Egyptian book he described and looked it up further. It turned out that the old Egyptian manuscript it reprinted was copied from a still earlier source and that it contained mathematical calculations I thought might be useful in increasing the strength of my transmitter. I was under the impression that it had been sent to me on approval and that I could quickly copy the calculations and return the book to the dealer. You can imagine my chagrin when I found he had already billed you for it."

"I couldn't leave it lying around the house for you to find it, and I couldn't bring myself to destroy such a valuable volume. Therefore, I donated it in your name to one of the university libraries, using some of the most technical provisions in your tax code to maximize its value to you as a charitable deduction. It shouldn't end up costing you very much, and I can more than re-coop your net loss if you allow mw to assist you in filling out your income tax returns this year. I have examined your last year's return and have found several ways I can reduce the amount you have to pay."

It was Hope's turn to feel embarrassed. She had to explain to Rasputin how she had refused to pay for the book she had not believed she had ordered, and how to the credit card company had agreed to cancel the debt. "The only ethical thing I can do now," she said more to herself than to the cat, "Is to write them apologizing for my error and enclosing a check for the cost of the book." Rasputin tactfully turned the conversation to other things.

Following this lengthy discussion, the close friendship between Hope and Rasputin reached new heights. Each evening, the cat would joyously welcome her arrival as before. She took to preparing dishes for dinner that she thought Rasputin would enjoy more than the dry cat food. Twice a week, she would order delivery of a pizza, which they would share. After dinner, they would settle together on the sofa, sharing a blanked, and watching news programs on TV.

The thing that Hope enjoyed about their new relationship was the ability to chat with Rasputin every evening as they had dinner. No longer obliged to conceal his ability to speak, Rasputin and Hope had lengthy discussions about foreign affairs. Hope was amazed to find that Rasputin had a much better knowledge of the subject than did the State Department officials with whom she worked each day. Their talks reminded her of the many conversations she had had with her parents on the subject before she had left home.

One evening, Hope returned home to find Rasputin waiting anxiously for her at the door. He leaped up and hugged her as he did every night, but she sensed his excitement.

"Wonderful news!" he told her. "I finally managed to contact Xilback Control today. They are sending a ship here to take me back to my home planet. There's only one trouble," he added, his voice becoming sorrowful. "I shall hate to leave you."

Hope's heart fell at hearing the news of the cat's imminent departure. "Isn't there some way you could stay here with me? I'd even eat pizza for dinner every night with you if that would induce you not to leave me."

"I wish I could stay," he said sorrowfully. "But I have an obligation to return home and brief them about conditions on earth. I can't shirk my responsibilities."

"Possibly I could go with you," Hope said tentatively.

"That would be possible," he answered, "The space ship has enough room to carry you back, too. And if you go with me, I will make sure you enjoy living with me on my planet even more than I did enjoy living with you here. But you should know that earth is so distant from my planet that communications are difficult. If you accompany me, you would have to prepare to remain there for some time. Hope sat down and began to review her options.

The next day, Hope's employees were surprised to find her not at her desk when they arrived at the office. She almost always was the first one to arrive. By noon, she had still not turned up. This was most unusual. She always notified them beforehand if she was taking leaving or otherwise be absent and had appointed one of her unit chiefs to act for her in her absence. On the following day, she was still absent. Phone calls to her home elicited no response. Finally, her employees felt they had to notify State Department Security of her absence.

On the next day, two State Department Security officials came to her house. When she did not answer the bell, they tried the door and found it unlocked. The house, when they entered, was clearly vacant. All Hope's things were in order; there were no signs of violence. Subsequent calls to her banks revealed no large cash withdrawals or other indications of a planned departure. Frustrated, the officials notified the Washington police, who conducted the usual missing persons' type investigation. They, too, could come up with no explanation for Hope's disappearance. Hope has still not returned, and the case remains in the open investigation file of the Washington police.

There is only one footnote to this story. On his birthday this year, Hope's father found a letter from her in hi mailbox. The handwriting on the envelop was clearly Hope's. Surprisingly, the envelop bore no postage stamp and was crumbled, as though it had traveled a long way. In the letter within, Hope expressed her best birthday wishes to her father. She added that she was on an extended vacation and was having a wonderful time. She would fill her parents in on the details when she got back home.

When he returned the letter to the envelope, Hope's father saw what appeared to be a long hair at the bottom of the envelop. He took it out and examined it. It resembled a cat's whisker but was far longer than any whisker had ever seen on a cat. On a whim, he gave the whisker to one of his colleagues, a biology professor, and asked him if he could properly identify the hair. The Biology professor came to his office the next day, returning the hair. "This is the damnedest thing," he said. "Where did you get it? I examined it carefully. I would swear that its molecular structure is different from anything that has ever been reported."

Homo Superior

The discovery while excavating for an extension of the Alaska oil pipeline of a perfectly preserved body of an ancient human went largely unnoticed. Although in a much better state of preservation that such previous finds, which fact in itself was not particularly newsworthy. However, when laboratory examination of the specimen indicated that the find could conceivably be not that of a human being but possibly that of a more advanced species, it initiated a cascade of news coverage and intense scientific debate.

The evidence that it was not human was initially attacked as flimsy. The fact that three of its front teeth were much smaller than the others and appeared to represent new teeth formation in an adult could be written off as an anomaly. So could the fact that the specimen's brain had more than double the number of found in the largest human brain on record. It was only when detailed analysis of the creature's DNA became available that it could be definitively identified as that of a totally different species. The press dubbed the find homo superior," and the name stuck.

The acceptance of the archeological find as that of the remains of a hitherto unknown species and a species superior to man launched a storm of debate. Many scientists argued in favor of DNA testing of all living humans to determine if any had the DNA elements differentiating them from Homo Sapiens and if there were any pure home superiors who survived, although this latter possibility was deemed to be highly unlikely. A small group of scientists asserted that if any such individuals could be found they might provide the basis needed for genetic engineering to produce a race of pure home superiors. This proposal was in turn attacked as advocating fascism and racism. Conservative leaders of all major religious groups argued that only God had the right to create life and that any effort at genetic engineering would be blasphemy.

In the midst of the controversy, a group of eleven individuals gathered together in a remote chateau in Nice, France. They had been summoned to discuss the find and were seated around a large circular table. Rather than speaking, they communicated telepathically, both for speed and to eliminate the possibility of their being overheard.

Opinions of what to do varried widely. At length, they decided it was time to vote, their standard procedure. The joint resolution was proposed and seconded and carried by a tally of nine to one, with one of them choosing to abstain. It provided that the group would do nothing to call the attention of human beings to their existence and that they would do nothing in response to the discovery. Having voted, they agreed to follow the matter closely and to gather again if the situation warranted it. They then said goodbye to each other and adjourned.

The individuals then all went off to make their travel arrangements to return to their respective homes. Three of them had come from North America, but they traveled separately because of their different places of residence. One was to return to the United States. He was the one member who had voted against the resolution, favoring the decision to do nothing to call their existence, but strongly opposing the plan to do nothing. He also possessed the highest intelligence of the group, although he was adroit in keeping this hidden.

This individual believed that God had created them with the intention that they would use their superior intelligence and other gifts for their own benefit and that of mankind. As he boarded his plane, he had already made his decision. When he reached home, he would go into politics and obtain the presidential nomination. He had not yet decided which party he would choose as his political vehicle, but he had absolutely no doubt that he would be successful in using his abilities to win both the nomination and the presidency of the United States.

The Perfect Drug

The Mercedes Pharmaceutical Company was uniquely favored among the host of new drug company startups located in California by the fact that its principal scientific advisor was a winner of the Nobel Prize in Medicine. It easily raised hundreds of millions of dollars from hedge funds and other private investors and commenced work on s score of research projects, including on a vaccine to prevent all forms of cancer and a cure for Alzheimer's disease. Its most promising project, however, was the drug labeled "Formula 480."

This unique drug had been formulated according to new protocols devised by the company. These gave highest priority in the design of any new drug to one that would provide the highest profit if it were successful. In most cases, this required both a high profit margin for each individual dose as well as the merchandizing of a high volume of the drug. "Formula 480" met both these requirements superbly.

Another valuable feature of the new drug was that the processes involved in its formulation were incredibly complex. They would defy efforts of generic drug firms to duplicate them after the patent obtained by Mercedes for the product expired. Finally, "Formula 480's" ingredients were all inert, eliminating the harmful side effects caused by virtually all pharmaceutical products. This important factor meant that in advertizing it on TV, Mercedes would not have to waste valuable time in its commercials by rapidly mentioning in an inaudible voice all of the possible harmful side effects that might come from using the product.

Progress on the development of "Formula 480"proved to be so promising that Mercedes decided to abort its other research projects and devote all available funds to work on the project. Over the side went the two anti cancer vaccines, which had already reached the late trial stage, as well as a cure for Alzheimer's. Hundreds of millions more dollars came from hedge funds and private investors eager to reap the great rewards promised from partial ownership in "Formula 40."

There was only one small flaw in the plan. Being totally inert, of what use was the new drug? This was a problem, but fortunately not an unsolvable one. The answer was to create a totally new disease, for which large and repeated doses of "Formula 480" were the only effective treatment.

The large research staff of Mercedes quickly sprang into action. They worked long and hard, but to no avail. Sadly, it was determined that every part of the human body, from the brain on top to the big toe on the bottom were already subject to known diseases and congenital physical malformation or breakdown in functioning. In short, no new ailment for which "Formula 480" was the answer could be found or created.

Panic raged in the halls of the Mercedes complex. Employees, particularly senior management, saw their potentially lucrative stock options change into worthless pieces of paper. Hedge funds began liquidating their holdings in the company and taking the huge tax losses the beneficial income tax provisions for the financial sector available to them. Fortunately, the Mercedes Board of Directors proved up to meeting the problem. The first step it took was to downgrade the position of the principal scientific advisor, placing him under the supervision of the vice president for administration. It then established the post of chief advertizing adviser and recruited for it the winner of the newly instituted Nobel Prize in Advertizing.

The new advisor, usually described in the press as the "twenty-three year old advertizing genius" quickly solved the problem. He identified the previously undetected problems of "Placebo Disease," the varying maladies afflicting a sizeable number of individuals who are placed in the test groups used to judge the effectiveness of new drugs. Those who scoffed at the so-called melody were quickly won over by the mass of scientific data provided by independent researchers carefully chosen by Mercedes confirming the disposition of highly emotional individuals to suffer ill effects from placebos

Marketed to the public under the trade name Wonderfulla, "Formula 480" s ales boomed after its quick approval by the Federal Drug Administration. Soon watchers of every TV station and cable channel were bombarded during the commercial breaks in programs inserted every five minutes of the serious threat to life stemming from" Placebo Disease . Actors appearing at the brink of death were shown miraculously recovered and in the best of health after being administered Wonderfulla.

Following a bitter contest between the New York Stock Exchange and NASDAQ over which exchange would be privileged to list the stock, Mercedes went public in an initial stock offering so large that it dwarfed anything else that year. Bidding for the new issue stock was so great that the underwriting firms allotted most of it to influential members of Congress and to senior officials of a few favored financial institutions.

All those involved in any way with the company became very rich. The underwriting firms reported much higher annual profits for that year thanks to the underwriting, and their senior executives received even higher than usual annual bonuses. All those lucky enough to be able to purchase the stock at or soon after it went public saw their investment triple overnight and then triple again. Every employee of Mercedes became at least a multimillionaire thanks to the stock option they had been furnished without charge, with senior management becoming billionaires due to their larger number of stock options.

Within a few months of going public, the Board of Directors showed their financial acumen, purchasing a small, neighborhood pharmacy in North Ireland. Mercedes accomplished this through a reverse takeover, thereby officially transforming itself from a US firm to one located in the United Kingdom. As a result of this change in status, Mercedes, now known as Mercedes-Jones Ltd., is babble to shelter from American taxes a very high part of its profits earned abroad.

Today the case of Mercedes-Jones Ltd. Is studied at every business school in the county as an illustration of how sound, enlightened management can advance the creation of wealth in the United States. It is truly a story to make every American proud.

Limbo

The first sensation William Morrison had was one of floating on a
body of water. He struggled to open his eyes, and when he succeeded, he found he was lying flat on the deck of what seemed to
be a wooden boat. Raising himself up, he saw the boat was indeed
on a body of water, the extent of which he could not ascertain because of a dense fog on all sides. The boat appeared to be moving
at a slow but steady pace through the water. The stern of the boat
was enveloped in fog; he saw no crew member, sails and heard no
engine, so that he had no idea of what was propelling the craft.

After some period, Morrison saw what seemed to be land in
the distance. The boat moved steadily forward and it became clear
that what he saw was indeed land. A white sandy beach along the
shore gave rise further inland to a peak covered with trees. There
were no traces of human habitation. The boat touched gently on
the sand and stopped. Nothing happened. After a few minutes,
Morrison climbed out of the boat and cautiously took a few steps.

Turning to reassure himself that the boat was still there, he was
horrified to see it had silently departed and was now disappearing
into the fog. He had no choice. Apparently he was marooned here,
whether for good or evil he knew not...Having no other alternative, he decided to explore. Possibly he might find some civilization, though that appeared too unlikely. Morrison saw no birds

or any other form of animal life. Curiously, all of the vegetation seemed to be of a single type, each some dozen feet tall and bearing a reddish fruit he had never seen before.

Morrison found that he was famished. He was tempted to taste the strange fruit, but decided not to because it might be poisonous. He wished that there were some birds around since if he saw them eating the fruit; he could be reasonably sure it would not harm him, Further on; he encountered a small stream, rapidly flowing down from the mountain into the sea. He knelt and tasted it. The water was clear and cold. At least, he thought, he would not suffer from thirst.

He continued along the beach until reached a point at which a high ridge ran down from the mountain to the sea, making further progress impossible. He thought of ascending the mountain, but decided to postpone it for another today, hopefully after he had found something to eat. Returning the way he had come, he was heartened and excited when he saw a round thatch hut a short way off beyond the beach under some of the trees. There was no sign of any inhabitant, and when he approached and entered it, he found the hut completely bare. No furniture, no implements, no sign that anyone else had ever been there. Who had made it, since it clearly could not have made itself or put together by nature, was a mystery.

Exhausted, Morrison entered the hut and collapsed on the floor. He was drained of all energy, at the end of his room. He was bewildered by what had happened to him. He had been in his office working all morning, then decided to go for a leisurely lunch at his club. His last conscious memory before waking up in that mysterious boat was of entering the elevator in his office building to descend to the street. Surprisingly the ground that constituted the floor of the hut was reasonably comfortable. All in all, he was more comfortable than he had been while sleeping in his shelter half while on bivouac in the army. He curled up in a fetal position and, still hungry, fell asleep.

When he awakened, the sun was shining into the hut. He felt refreshed from the stress of the previous day but even hungrier than before. Setting out to look for food, he saw nothing he could possibly eat other than the strange fruit hanging from every tree. He found the spring and had some water that helped assuage his hunger. As he walked back to his hut, he went over in his mind the possibility of eating a small bit of the red fruit, hopefully not enough to seriously harm him.

Suddenly he saw the hut. His first thought was that it was his own. Then he spotted a human figure sitting on the ground in front of it. Morrison was overjoyed and ran toward it, looking forward to being able to talk to a fellow human being and hopefully of learning more about this strange place. He cried "hello," but there was no response, no sign the individual had heard him. Finally, now so close to the man that he could touch him, Morrison said again "hello," adding to introduce himself "my name is Bill Morrison."

No answer. The man simply sat there, staring fixedly ahead. In case he was deaf, Morrison tapped him lightly on the shoulder. Still no response. Finally in desperation Morrison asked as loudly as he could "Do you have a name?"

The man turned to face him, "Yes, I do," he said in a flat, emotionless voice without looking at Morrison. Looking closely at this enigmatic figure, Morrison concluded that he was about Morrison's own age, in his mid forties. He was wearing a three- piece business suit and a striped tie. Morrison had been similarly dressed when he awakened in the boat, but had doffed coat, tie and vest in his hut because of heat.

"What is your name? Morrison asked, wondering if for some reason the man responded only to a direct question.

"John Baxter," came back the response, uttered in the same toneless voice.

"Do you know where we are?

"Yes," came back the answer.

Morrison thought this was a lot like playing some silly party game. "All right," he asked, "Where are we?"

"In limbo."

Morrison thought he must have heard something else. How could he be in limbo? As far as he recalled, Limbo was supposedly a place, not Heaven and not Hell, where the souls of babies who had died before they could be baptized went. "Do you mean we are dead? He asked, fearing the answer.

"Yes."

"Good God," said aloud, despite himself. How could it be true? Such things couldn't really happen. But apparently they did, he realized. That would explain a lot of the mystery about how he got here.

"All right," he said. "If we're really dead, why are we here? I thought when you died your are supposed to go either to Heaven or to Hell."

"We've come back," the same monotonous voice he had come to detest "Because when we were alive we never did enough good things to permit us to enter Heaven nor enough bad ones to result in our being sent down to the damned souls in Hell."

This was the longest utterance Baxter had made to date, but certainly no more welcome than his previous ones.

"How long have you been here?" Morrison inquired.

"Forever." Obviously Baxter was speaking rhetorically rather than literally. The business suit he was wearing was of a style that could not have possibly been made before the end of the Second World War.

"How long will I be here?"Morrison asked.

"I don't know, probably forever."

Is there any way I can get out of here?" Morrison asked desperately. From what he had seen of Limbo, it could hardly be worse than Hell.

"Not that I know of," from Baxter, still that toneless reply.

It was excruciating trying to have a conversation with Baxter.

Morrison could not understand how any person could be so un-willing to engage with a fellow human being, particularly when in a situation such as they shared. He wondered if Baxter was simply in a severely depressed state now or whether he had behaved in the same way, when alive.

He knew he wanted to get away. Even being alone was prefer-able. He had one final question. "Are there any other people here in Limbo beside the two of us?"

"Yes."

"How many?"

"Where are they?"

"I don't know."

Morrison turned and started to leave. Then he realized he had one question he had to ask. "What is there to eat here?"

"The red fruit on the trees."

It's not poisonous>"

"No."

Without another word, Morrison turned away and headed back to where he believed his hut was located. He was relieved to not have to talk further with Baxter. It was even worse than being alone in this God-forsaken place. On the way back, he stopped to stare at the fruit on the trees. He wondered if Baxter was correct in stating it was not harmful, whether he was telling him the truth or attempting to deceive him for some mysterious motive. He de-cided it was most unlikely was deliberately lying, his demeanor, his body language all strongly indicating he was speaking the truth, at least as far as he understood it.

Morrison reached up and took a small handful of the red fruit. He tasted a bit and cautiously waited to see if there was any unfa-vorable reaction. There was none. He took more and ate enough to appease his hunger. He disliked the texture, which was mushy, but in its favor it had a slightly sweet taste, much he supposed you would get if you ate a raw sweet potato. All told; he would have described the food as neither good nor bad, simply acceptable.

After some delay and concern he found his way back to his hut. He could think of nothing further to do. Certainly, attempting to converse with Baxter was so difficult it was better off being alone. He entered his cut, curled up and fell asleep. His last waking thought was that the red fruit was just like everything else in Limbo except for Baxter, neither good nor bad, just adequate.

Morrison fell into the same routine each day. He would get up early, walk to the stream for a drink and then go to one of the trees for his food. While alive he had enjoyed three meals a day and so ate on that same schedule here. After each meal, he would return to his hut and sleep. It was extremely boring, but there was simply nothing else to do. On none of these occasions did he ever encounter a person and he was never once tempted to visit Baxter.

One day while walking to the stream he saw a hut. His first impression was that he had mistakenly taken a path to Baxter. Morrison was about to turn away when he heard the sound of someone weeping. It seemed strange for Baxter to express so much emotion. Then he realized it could not be Baxter. The voice was undoubtedly that of a woman.

Morrison approached the hut and within that there was indeed a woman weeping horribly, interrupted by occasional curses. Without stopping to reflect, he crouched to enter the hut, picked her up and wrapped his arms around her, trying somehow to comfort her. He realized that his sudden appearance might be alarming and so said in as friendly a tone as he could, "Hi, my name is Bill Morrison, is there anything I can do for you?" She stopped weeping, pulled herself away, turned and stared at him, her expression showing her fear.

Morrison smiled and repeated what he had just told her. She relaxed slightly. "Hi," she said cautiously. My name is Theresa White. My friends call me Terry." Her voice was very attractive, as was she. Morrison guessed her age as about forty. She had blond hair, eyes that appeared green, and was wearing a stylish suit.

He was about to shake her hand, and then thought better of it.

He didn't want to frighten her.

"It's a pleasure to have you here," he said. "Is there anything I can do to help you?" he repeated.

"Where are we?" she asked. "How did I get here?"

Trying to sound as confident as he could to reassure her he briefly summarized what Baxter had told him

"That can't be true," she said softly. "I'm only forty-three. No one does so young. I wasn't sick at all. I have a husband and two young children. Why my daughter is just eight years old."

"I was just forty-six when I apparently died. I was not sick either." He explained about leaving his office for lunch and awakening to find himself on that mysterious boat."

"That same thing happened to me," she said. "I also awakened to find myself on that boat that came up to the shore and then slipped away when I go off. It's still hard to believe that there's a real Limbo," she added. "Could you take me to Baxter and listen for myself to what he says. Isn't it possible you didn't properly understand what he told you?"

Morrison thought of attempting to persuade her not to go. Trying to speak with Baxter might throw her back into a funk. Still, she had a right to listen to him herself. And while he thought what Baxter had told him was so absurd it was possible he had somehow misunderstood the man. "By all means," he said, "It might be better if you listened to him yourself. Let's go there now.

As he led her in the direction of Baxter's hut they passed some of the trees and he stopped. "If you are as hungry as I was when I arrived here you probably want something to eat."

She smiled at him gratefully. "Yes, I do," she said. "I'm famished."

Morrison picked some of the red fruit and gave her most of it; eating a small quantity of it himself to show her it was safe to do so. "How do you like it?" He asked.

"It's odd tasting. I never had anything like it before. What kind of fruit is it?"

"I don't know either," Morrison replied. "I think it's only found here in Limbo. "

She finished the fruit and said, "I would say it's OK."

"That's the way I feel about it. I always tell myself is adequate. He smiled. "In fact adequate is the word I'd use to describe everything in Limbo. Except you," headed. "You're perfect."

"Good God," he thought to himself. "Am I flirting with her?" He didn't want to appear too forward, so he quickly changed the subject, asking her about herself. She didn't seem to notice his abrupt change in the tenor of his conversation and told him that she had been a high school biology teacher.

"You know, "she added, "I seem to remember being in a car going to my school. Do you think I might have been killed in an auto accident?"

"It's possible," he answered, "Or it could just as easily have been a sudden stroke. You can't tell because it apparently makes no difference about how you look or feel here."

He thought of warning her again about Baxter's likely attitude toward her, then reconsidered. He didn't want to bias her opinion of the man.

After several mistakes, he finally found the correct path to Baxter's. They found Baxter sitting in his usual place in front of the hut staring fixedly ahead.

"Hi, Baxter," Morrison called out, attempting sound cheerful. "I've brought someone to meet you. Her name is Terry White."

Terry stepped forward and stuck out her hand to shake Baxter's. He continued to stare ahead, ignoring her.

"I'm very glad to meet you," she said."

Again, no response from Baxter. "You see what I mean," Morrison whispered to her. To get any answer, you have to ask him a direct question."

"Is your name Baxter?"

"Yes."

"Where are we?"

"In Limbo."

"How did we get here?"

"We died."

"Am I dead?"

"Yes."

"How long will I be here?"

"Forever."

Morrison could sense that Terry was becoming increasingly annoyed and frustrated by Baxter's behavior. "Don't you think it might be time for us to leave?" He asked. "It's about time for us to have something to eat."

She remained quiet for a few seconds, and then nodded her head in agreement. "Yes," she said. Then turning to leave, she went down and thanked Baxter for his courteous assistance. Morrison wondered if she was polite or just sarcastic. As she turned to accompany him, he was startled to see out of the corner of his eye Baxter turn his head and stare at her. "So the old boy does have an eye for the ladies," he told himself, although he said nothing to Terry about it.

On the way back to Terry's hut, Morrison asked her what her reaction was to Baxter's comments. "It's just as you said," she answered. "I think he's telling the truth. Any you were perfectly right. He's insufferable."

They reached her hut, sat down and chatted in friendly fashion. She told him more about herself, about her students, about how much she enjoyed the year off from teaching when she had been awarded a fellowship to take some advanced courses in biology at the university. He, in turn, talked about himself, about his wife Irene and their two sons, about his work as an economic consultant to firms in the construction industry. He found her a most charming woman, wonderful to talk to and very attractive.

They broke off only to get another meal from the fruit trees, stopped for a drink at the stream and returned to her to resume chatting. Morrison suddenly realized it was getting late, and the sun was close to setting. "I'd better leave now," he said. "I want to get back to my hut before it's too dark for me to find my way."

As he stood to leave she reached out her arms and grabbed him. "Please don't leave me she said. I don't want to alone in this awful place. Please stay here."

Morrison didn't have the heart to say no. He sat down again and smiled cheerful at her. He realized all the risks in becoming too involved with Terry, both because of the bizarre conditions in which they were living and because he had known her for less than a day. They continued the friendly conversation until the sun went down. Then they entered Terry's hut and lay down to sleep.

"Good night, Bill," she said, turning to sleep on her side. He thought her voice very sweet. In reminded him a lot of his wife. "Good night, Terry," he answered in reply, adding "Sleep tight," as he always had told Irene.

During the night, the temperature dropped appreciably; Morrison awakened feeling very cold, his teeth almost chattering. Terry t turned to face him. "I'm freezing," she said, "Isn't there something we can do?" He turned over to face her, asked her to turn on her other side and covering the back of her body with his own, put his arms around her and hugged her close. He could feel the increased warmth from the two bodies touching. "Thank you very much," she whispered. "You feel like a warm furnace. I 'm much warmer now." From her quiet breathing, he realized she was back asleep.

He lay there quietly, unable to sleep; his mind troubled my conflicting emotions. Although he had actually done nothing improper so far, he felt guilty as though he had already cheated on Irene. Morrison had had a few affairs before marriage, but in their twenty-two years of marriage, he had never touched another woman. And there was Terry to consider. She gave every indication of being very much in love with her husband.

His common sense told him something different. He was dead. Terry was dead. There was no chance he would ever see Irene again. She was such a warm, caring, unselfish person that she could never end up in Limbo. If anyone deserved a free pass to Heaven, it was his wife. Morrison finally fell asleep, his arms around Terry, smelling the aroma of her hair, feeling the warmth of her body.

When Morrison awakened, the sun was streaming through the hut entrance. He was still embracing Terry. She awakened, turned to face him, and gave him a cheerful good morning. Then she suddenly kissed him, hard and passionately. "Make love to me, Bill, "she said passionately, "Please, please make love to me."

All of his doubts fell away. He grabbed her hard, kissed her, and began ripping off his clothes. When he was naked, he tore off her clothing, Terry helping him to unhook her bra. He mounted her and made love to her, urgently. It felt wonderful. He hadn't had sex since he had died, and Terry was an extremely attractive woman. When he was spent and relaxed he was resting, he realized that somehow he had not enjoyed the love -making as much as he should have. Sex with his wife had almost always been a grand experience. This time it had been, to be put honestly, just average.

He looked at Terry and kissed her gently on the forehead. "That was great," he lied. "I hope you enjoyed it."

"It was wonderful," she said. He looked at the expression on her face and realized she was lying to make him feel better. He laughed. "Admit it," he said. "It was just average, just like everything else in this damned place."

Terry laughed, too. "You're right," she confirmed, "Just average.

That was the last time they had sex. They lived now, treating each other as the best of friends, sleeping side by side, enjoying every minute with the other, but never again being intimate. They exchanged confidences, spoke about their plans and dream when alive, of their families and their children. Each day was like the last. They ate the fruit from the trees, walked hand in hand along the beach, and sunned themselves on the sand.

Then one day, Morrison awakened with a scheme. 'Terry," he told her excitedly, "I think I may have come up with a way for us to get out of Limbo."

"What is it?" she asked eagerly. "I'd give anything to get out of here."

He explained that when they had seen Baxter, the latter had seemed fascinated by her. "As a man, he explained," I certainly can tell when another man is interested in an attractive woman. And you are much more than just attractive and for Baxter to display any interest in anything is totally out of character."

"How do you suggest we use that to get out of Limbo?"

"Like this," he explained."We fix you up so that you look sexy, voluptuous, and lascivious. You go there and try and seduce Baxter. I think that it would be easy."

"That's fine," she said, her interest fading. "So he lays me. How does that help us?"

"No, he doesn't actually lay you," Morrison answered."I go with you and hide behind some trees so he doesn't see me. When you get him hot and ready to have sex with you, you pull back and refuse. Hopefully, he will try to rape you. You shout for help and I come running to your aid, like the hero in the old melodrama rescuing the heroine from a fate worse than death."

"And how does that help us?" she asked doubtfully.

"Simple. If he really tries to rape you and you don't like the idea and refuse and I save you from rape, I will have done something good. Hopefully that will be enough to tip the balance and allow me to leave Limbo and get into Heaven."

"Even if that works, how does that help me?"

"Don't you get it?" Morrison asked. "If I am sprung and get to go to Heaven, you will have helped me. You also will have done something good, and can accompany me to Heaven."

She thought for a minute. "I suppose it's worth a try. We might as well get on with it.

Terry stood, took off her suit jacked, blouse and bra, then put on only her blouse. She buttoned only one button, managing to show most of her cleavage. She was so sexy looking Morrison found himself interested once again in having sex with her, although he knew the result would be just average. She then took off her skirt and panties, before putting the skirt. Hiking it up to show more off her thighs she removed it again and began ripping one of the seams.

"What are you doing?" he asked her. "You're ruing that skirt?" I'm putting in slit to make me look sexier. The new slit revealed more of her beautiful body than would be allowed on most public beaches. "If you're trying to do something hard," she explained, "My husband told me, go for broke. If you want me to seduce Baxter, let's go all the way."

Hand in hand, they headed off to Baxter's hut. "Switch your rear end when you see him, he advised. She wriggled her hips in a provocative fashion. "Like this," she asked with a smile. "Perfect," he answered. "If that doesn't attract Baxter, nothing will. They approached Baxter's hut and saw him as before, sitting on the ground and staring fixedly ahead. Morrison concealed himself behind a tree and Terry walked slowly toward the hut, wriggling her hips for all she was worth.

"Hello, Baxter, dear," she said, lowering her voice to make it sound sexier. "I want you. How would you like to help me?"

She sat down in front of him and bent over, her blouse opening to reveal her nipples. I have something on my back," she went on. "Can you look at it?"

She tugged at his arm. He looked up at her, and Morrison could see lust written all over his face. Baxter had said he had been in Limbo forever, clearly longer than had Morrison. If Baxter was in any way a man, and of that Morrison had no doubt, he would want to have sex with Terry. She half pulled; half led Baxter into the hut and removed her blouse. Hiding behind the tree, Morrison listened carefully for any cry for help. He had to wait for what seemed hours. He feared that Baxter had not attempted to rape Terry, or worse yet she had decided to try sex with him.

Finally, it came. He raced to the hut, saw Baxter naked

attempting to mount a naked Terry grabbed Baxter by the ankle and dragged him out of the hut. He hauled Baxter up to an erect position, then smashed him across the nose, knocking the man flat. He realized he had hit Baxter harder than he had intended, letting the animosity he felt toward the man have full rein He hoped he had not killed Baxter and was relieved when the later moaned, showing Morrison had not killed him.

Terry came out of the hut, rearranging her blouse and torn skirt. "I hope I got there in time," he said, "Fearful that he had not.

"I'm very happy to say that you just did," she said, kissing him on the cheek. They walked back, hand in hand to her hut, hoping that their plan had succeeded.

Morrison awakened. He was lying flat on his back. From the motion, he realized he was somehow back on that damned boat. He opened his eyes and confirmed he was. Anxiously he looked around, hoping to see Terry, but he was alone. Ass before the rear of the boat was obscured by a dense fog. He saw land in front of him, and as the boat neared it, he saw the terrain was just like that of Limbo. The familiar trees with the red fruit came close to the sandy beach. He stepped onto the sand and the boat silently slipped away back into the fog.

Superficially, nothing had changed. Whatever this place was it seemed identical to the Limbo he had left. He walked off, anxious to get to Terry's hut and learn if anything had happened to her. Try as he might, he couldn't find the hut. Then he heard a strange sound which he had never heard in Limbo. He neared the source of the sound, which sounded very much like crying. At length, he arrived at a large clearing. Before him were hundreds of infants and very young babies, all naked, all crying. There was a strong odor of human waste, logical in view of the fact that none of the infants was wearing diapers or was old enough to be toilet trained.

He turned away in disgust and walked away as quickly as he could. This was the place; he realized, where the infants who had died before they could be baptized were sent. He walked further, but as the wailing of the infants disappeared he now heard a new sound, the beating of drums. Wondering what the noise might be, found himself at another clearing. In front of him dancing in a circle were about thirty human figures of various shades of brown and tan, the men naked except for loin clothes, the women bare breasted and wearing grass skirts. More than a few of them had what appeared to be bones through their noses. They gyrated in tune to the beat of the drums he had heard.

Suddenly, the drums stopped their beat; the dancers stopped and prostrated themselves on the ground, all paying homage to the mountain that rose in front of them. These thought, Morrison, must be the adults who had never been baptized before they died.

He turned and ran away, heedless of where he was heading. Then he stopped, threw himself to the ground and began sobbing. He knew now, without any shadow of a doubt, that he was in Limbo, that there was more than one limbo and that he had lost Terry forever. He doubted if he would ever stop weeping. Morrison wept, both because he would never see Terry again and because no matter how he tried, he was damned forever to remain in Limbo.

Precepts Of Statesmanship

The precepts of effective statesman ship were best set down by Sir Edmund Chastleton, whose term in office is regarded by British historians as the happiest period in that nation's history. His principles are clear and concise and are available to readers through a brief memorandum he wrote in 1896. The first and cardinal precept is no matter how series the crisis to adhere steadfastly to a policy of total inaction. Sir Edmund at the start of every Cabinet meeting would remind his ministers that "Today's solution is tomorrow's problem." The wisdom of this policy is universely hailed by historians; in his seven years in office, Great Britain was involved in no major wars and scarcely any violence in the colonial areas.

Sir Edmund's second precept is that if forced by external events to take action, to do the least possible and to limit its extent only to what is necessary to create the illusion of a change in the original policy. The last principle is that after a short fixed period of time determined before the start of the action whether the change has been successful a failure, to declare complete victory and return to the previous status quo.

In a much longer appendix attached to his memorandum, Sir Edmund provided the source material showing the soundness of his precepts. He cited Napoleon's invasion of Russia in 1812,

President Abraham Lincoln's decision to attempt to resupply Fort Sumter in Charleston harbor in 1862, Hitler's invasion of Russia in 1941 and the United States invasion of Iraq in 2002, All these represented the destruction that could be inflicted on a country and its leadership by taking action when inaction would have been by far the wiser alternative.

Sir Edmund skillfully answered critics who pointed to what they claimed had been successful actions taken by governments. In the United States those attacking Sir Edmund's precepts pointed to the American Social Security System, which they asserted represented a vital guarantee of an adequate life- style to virtually all working Americans. Although Sir Edmund was no longer alive to refute this criticism personally, his defenders pointed out the section in his appendix. This dealt with the "apparent success" of some government actions that this was a result of the understandable error in judging the results over too short a period of time for the real failure of the program to become obvious. This position seems supported by recent warnings in the United States. The American Social Security System is rapidly going bankrupt. Current payers into the system will be unable by the time they retire to recoup in their monthly retirement payments anything like the cash the paid into it during their working lives.

It must be sadly admitted that the leaders of no major nation today formulate government policy in accordance with Sir Edmund's principles of statesmanship. Perhaps as world conditions continue their steady deterioration, the pendulum will swing back to the level of sanity that prevailed in Britain while Sir Edmund headed the government.

Civilized?

Major Eric Hansen limped along at the head of a column of perhaps a hundred survivors. He dragged his right foot, his ankle aching from the spear wound, putting much of his weight on a large branch he had cut down and fashioned into a type of crutch. Hansen was desperately tired. He longed to stop and throw himself down on the side of the trail to rest. But he had to go on. To give up would be to condemn himself and all of the men under his command to a sure and painful death.

The column was made up of all of those left out of the eight hundred men of the regiment who had set out from their base camp to repair the continent-wide electric fence, which kept out the Behemoths from the settled area of the planet, Broma Three. It had supposedly been a routine mission; they had accomplished it successfully more than a dozen times before and Colonel Miller, the regimental commander, had decided not to encumber the troops by taking with them the artillery pieces that were available in case of emergency. Hansen, who was a veteran of three years' service on Broma Three, had personally witnessed the carnage caused by a Behemoth attack. He attempted unsuccessfully to convince the colonel to take the artillery as a precaution, to no avail. Miller had only recently arrived on the planet and had never seen a Behemoth. To him, Hansen's caution appeared excessive and possibly revealed a lack of courage.

Behemoth'S were the dominant life form, at least in that part of the planet that had been explored. They were huge, about twice the size of the American buffalo or bison, which they somewhat resembled. They differed, however, from the buffalo in having a head and shoulders that looked vaguely human, as well as a thin appendage on each shoulder that functioned much like an arm. Normally, they killed their opponents by simply trampling them to death, but they were also skilled at hurling large spears, with razor sharp points. It was one of these spears that had hit Hansen's ankle.

When Behemoth's charged you, it was extremely difficult to stop them. They were capable of speeds of about sixty miles an hour, giving them a momentum which was unlikely to be stopped by rifle shots or even by fire from a machine gun. Flight was on foot was unlikely to be successful since they could keep this speed up for over an hour. No Behemoth carcass had even been obtained for dissection in a lab. However, quick cutting into the body of one, fortunately, killed in the charge had revealed to Hansen that their hearts and other vital organs were protected by folds of heavy skin that functioned very much like protective armor. Short of using artillery or flame throwers, it was almost impossible to stop a charging body of Behemoths. Only a lucky rifle shot in the eye or to one of the neck arteries might kill it in time to avoid being trampled to death.

To make matters worse, the Behemoths also possessed a high level of intelligence. They had the ability in any confrontation with troops to distinguish the officers and noncommissioned officers from the privates and to target them with their spears. Hansen was aware of this and when he had realized the Behemoths were about to attack, had removed his insignia of rank. In this way, he would avoid being a special target and face no more risk than any of the enlisted men under his command. He had ordered his subordinates to do so and advised Colonel Miller and the other officers to take the same precaution.

None had listened to him. The lieutenants, brave young men

just out of the academy, had had their heads filled with stories of valor and saw themselves as heroes. The rest had followed the Colonel's advice not to do so as it would lose confidence in their officers if they saw them shedding their badges of rank. Hansen personally believed it would be worse for their efficiency to see all of their officers killed by Behemoth spears, but prudently said nothing. As a result of their false bravery, all of the other officers had been killed or mortally wounded by the end of the first two Behemoth charges, which the regiment had barely been able to repulse.

With their machine gun ammunition expended, and only rifle fire left to defend themselves, Hansen realized that the fate was already settled. He ordered the men to attempt to hit the Behemoths in the eye, but for even the best marksmen it would be an extremely difficult shoot. The third Behemoth charge easily broke through, with the men trampled left and right.

Hansen's position temporarily saved his life. He was on the right flank, and the Behemoths after breaking the line had pivoted and surged like an unstoppable tide toward the left flank, trampling the men unmercifully. A few shots rang out, but most simply turned and fled. Hansen knew he could not aid the. All that was left was to order his men to retreat as rapidly as possible. They had done so, but Hansen knew their reprieve was only temporary. Once they finished off the left flank, the Behemoths could very easily catch up with the survivors and finish them off in turn.

Given the obvious difficulties in maintaining a human presence of Broma Three, Hansen seriously doubted it was worth it. True, the explored part of the planet held extremely rich gold deposits which apparently could be economically mined and transported by spacecraft to Earth. The mines were operated both by individual prospectors and by several large mining companies. After several reverses, the military had succeeded in driving the Behemoths out of what became the populated area by using aircraft. Artillery and flame throwers. The area cleansed of Behemoths was then hopefully protected by the continent-wide fence and a capital established at Broma City, which housed the necessary government infrastructure and the transportation facilities for shipping the mined gold back to Earth. Hansen doubted that the decision to colonize Broma Three would have been made if it had been realized at the time that strong winds and dust storms would prevent the use of aircraft for much of the year. This would require maintenance of the fence to be accomplished by foot troops on the ground.

Hansen's thoughts were interrupted by shots behind him and some rifle firing. He realized that the Behemoths most have caught up with the tail of the column, and it was now their turn to be trampled. He thought of ordering them to turn and form a defensive line, but decided that would only hasten their deaths. "Retreat!" he ordered, "Retreat as rapidly as you can!" He knew as he gave the order that it was useless. Then he saw what appeared to be a gully or creek some distance ahead. Possibly, then men might be protected from the Behemoth charge by hunkering down to the depression. The Behemoths were so large that they had some difficulty in using their strength in confined areas.

Hansen moved as fast as he could toward the possible sanctuary of the gully. In the interest of speed, he discarded his stick and ran, suffering the pain from his ankle. Reaching the gully, he threw himself into it and aimed his rifle ahead, ready to fire at any Behemoth that became aware of him. Other survivors reached the gully and threw themselves into it. A quick glance up and down the depression showed him that at least twenty of the men had made it.

The last thing Hansen remembers was the sight of a line of Behemoths charging the depression and of firing a rifle at one of them, hoping desperately to hit it in the eye. He regained consciousness and opened his eyes. He was staring directly into the face of a Behemoth.

"I see that you are awake, Earthman," it said. The pronunciation was strange, but the words understandable. Hansen saw that he was in the same gully. To the right there was a pile of human corpses, dead soldiers who had been trampled to death.

"We have decided to spare your life temporarily," the beast said. "We have never had the opportunity to study you. We want to learn why humans behave as you do."

"What do you mean?" Hansen asked. He was truly mystified. This was not the way he expected these monsters to behave.

'Your behavior is baffling to us," the creature said. "You come to our world; you kill us with powerful weapons, you drive us from our lands, you dig holes in the ground and extract a yellow metal that is too soft to be good for anything. You began shooting at us today when we were busy looking for food and had done nothing to harm you."

Strange as his words were, Hansen realized that they had a certain amount of logic. From the Behemoth's point of view, the humans had behaved barbarously. He had a thought. "Could you tell me what you eat?"

"Why of course. We eat plants and vegetables. What do humans eat?"

In a flash, it became clear to Hansen the reason for the behavior of both humans and Behemoths. "Let me explain," he began slowly. "On this planet, you are the dominant life form. On Earth man is. We believe we are the only species capable of reason and that every other life form on the planet has been put there for our use and convenience. We eat some animals for food, others we raise and kill for clothing. In our past, we used to ride some for transportation."

The Behemoth, Hansen could no longer think of him as a beast, shuddered with repugnance. "Eat another animal," it said, unable to believe this.

"Even worse, there is an animal species on Earth somewhat similar in appearance to you. It does not have a high level of intelligence. At one stage in our history, they were slaughtered just for their skins. Naturally, when the first men from Earth saw you, they immediately concluded you were like the Earth buffalo, and could be treated just as humans treated the buffalo.

The Behemoth struggled with his emotions and finally regained his composure. "Now that you realize we are a species at least as civilized as Earthmen, can you convince the others of that fact. If we do not kill you but release you, would you return to your kind and tell them the true facts about us. Perhaps we can reach an agreement to coexist peacefully. If you remove that fence, stop trying to kill us and allow us to look for food in this area, there is no reason for us to ask you to stop digging holes in the ground and extracting that yellow metal.

Hansen wanted very much to live was about to answer the Behemoth that he would be happy to undertake the mission. But he simply could not, even to save his life. The Behemoth had been honest with him. He just couldn't lie in return.

"I'm afraid it wouldn't work," he said regretfully. They would never believe me. They would think I had gone crazy and lock me up. It would be even worse if they did believe I was speaking the truth. They would regard you as even more dangerous to their survival, both here on to all of the humans on Earth. Because human nature is so vile, they could not understand that life form could behave decently to them."

The Behemoth nodded his head in agreement. I am afraid Earthman that you are correct. We had already assumed that but wanted to give you a chance to tell us your views."

Hansen bowed his head and waited for the words condemning him to death. He could not blame them. They would be acting logically. He only hoped it would be quick and painless. .He was surprised when he heard the Behemoth say, "All right, Earthman; we will release you. You are free to return to your kind." Hansen was amazed at hearing these words, but the Behemoth went on to explain. "Killing you would not reduce the menace your kind is to us. And you appear far more civilized in your behavior than the people from your planet we have encountered thus far. It would simply be irrational for us to kill you without purpose."

Hansen gravely expressed his thanks. He also pledged that he would never lift his hand against the Behemoths again, in the army or elsewhere, but would instead do anything he could to modify man's treatment of them. The Behemoths cared for his wound, putting a poultice on it which overnight greatly reduced the swelling and pain. The next morning, true to their word, Hansen was pointed in the right direction and set free.

Two days later, Hansen stumbled into a base camp and was cared for by the startled garrison. As he had decided to do on his journey, Hansen remained silent about his conversation with the Behemoth, stating only that the regiment had been attacked and overrun when their ammunition was exhausted. He described the retreat of the survivors and told his sympathetic interrogators that they had been overtaken and killed. He had survived; he explained, through blind luck by being hidden in a ditch under the dead bodies of some of the others.

After a few days of rest, Hansen was transported back to Broma City and interrogated events on the wiping out of the regiment. To his satisfaction, they seemed satisfied by his story. After a short period of rest in a resort maintained by the army, he was awarded a medal for valor, promoted to the rank of lieutenant colonel, and posted to another regiment. To everyone's surprise, he expressed his gratitude but submitted his resignation, stating that he had decided to return to Earth and go into another profession.

Hansen was given a luxury cabin when he departed Broma Three on the first spacecraft that carried passengers back to Earth. He had already decided he would enter government service or seek political office. Hopefully, he would be successful in gaining enough clout to be able to modify the treatment given by humans to the Behemoths on Broma Three as well as to the various animal species on Earth. In his mind, there was absolutely no doubt that when comparing human beings with Behemoths, which species was more civilized.

Admiralty Affairs

The Earl of Brundell was probably the least qualified person in England to be named First Lord of the Admiralty. Nonetheless, he was chosen for the post because the British Cabinet concluded his support was necessary if it was to retain power. In making the selection they ignored the fact that the Earl's sea sickness was so severe that he could not stand to be on board a ship, even one docked in the harbor. An even greater defeat was his total lack of common sense.

Brundell's unsuitability for the position became clear within a fortnight of his taking office, when he ordered that the three new men of war to be christened be named H.M.S. Torpid, H.M.S. Turgid and H.M.S. Timorous. To the cries of outrage from the naval officers under him, he declared that torpid, turgid and timorous were all perfectly fine words found in the Oxford Dictionary, and he would tolerate no opposition.

Worse was to follow. The Earl decided that since French men of war possessed forecastles, the English would do them one better, with sixcastles in the bow of the vessel. This fifty percent increase in the height of the superstructure made the vessels top heavy, subject capsize in the slightest heavy seas.

Unable to convince the Earl of the stupidity of this change in ship design, the British admirals took the only course open to them. They ordered the men of war of the British fleet to remain at anchor in their home ports. Eventually, they knew, Brundell would leave officce, at which time they could scrap the vessels he designed and replace them with efficient fighting vessels.

With the navy effectively removed from operations, Britain quickly lost its position as mistress of the seas. First to go was the vital supply line to India. Bombay and Calcutta were evacuated as the British forces could no longer defend them from French naval attacks, and the British garrisons were withdrawn to the greater safety of Delhi.

Next to be lost was British naval superiority in the Mediterranean. The British colonies of Malta and Cyprus had to surrender. Gibraltar managed to hold out, but only due to the skill of the governor in purchasing supplies from nearby Spanish towns.

At length, the Cabinet was forced to face the fact of Brundell's appalling stupidity and of the destruction he was wrecking on Britain's vital interests. He had to be replaced as First Lord of the Admiralty. But how" The Cabinet believed it still needed his political support.

After considerable discussion, it was decided to promote him from First Lord of the Admiralty to be prime minister. Although theoretically a post of greater power, the ministers decided that he would do less harm there. The various ministers, they decided, would render him harmless by taking charge of affairs in their own departments. The sitting prime minister graciously retired to pave the way for Brundell's elevation.

Little did they realize that in addition to being incredibly stupid, Brundell was also extremely energetic? Far from becoming a figurehead as prime minister, he grabbed all power into his own hands and began to exercise it fully, with no discretion.

What had happened to the British fleet was repeated in the country at general. Farmers rebelled at the mishandling of agricultural prices. Riots erupted in London and other major cities over the lack of food supplies. Bullion flowed from Britain in a torrent, and the Bank of England was rescued from bankruptcy only by the pawning of the crown jewels. The hapless sovereign locked himself into Buckingham Palace and pretended to be mad. In Scotland and Wales, demands for independence from England rose in a crescendo.

It was clear that if Brundell remained prime minister for much longer, the destruction he was inflicting could never be reversed. The Cabinet met in secret to discuss the best way of removing him. The time-honored means used to remove incompetent prime ministers, elevating them to the House of Lords, could not be employed to Brundell's case because he already was an Earl.

Finally, a solution was found. He was named Viceroy to India and quickly hustled on board vessels that was conveniently heading to the subcontinent in the fervent hope that it would be intercepted and Brundell made captive by a French man of war. The new prime minister summoned representatives of the parties in Parliament to a secret gathering. There, they jointly agreed that while they could in the future name incompetents to be prime minister, it would always be a lazy one who would undertake no new policies.

And so it has been. Many incompetents have served as British Prime Minister, but never an energetic one. At the next general election, Brundell's party was decisively defeated. Today, as a result of his performance, it is now defunct. You will look hard in British history to find any mention of the Earl of Brundell or of his party, so thoroughly have the British deliberately written him out of their history.

Unfortunately, when the thirteen British colonies gained independence from Great Britain and formed the United States of America, the story of the Earl of Brundell did not carry across the Atlantic. After some year of capable presidents, the United States in recent years is observing the harmful effects in this country of presidents who have been both incompetent and energetic.

Double Jeopardy

W. Langdon Smuthers lived in the nicest residence in Hell. It was not only centrally air- conditioned, but had four bedrooms, a massive dining room, a book- lined library, a swimming pool and a tennis court. Those who saw it could not understand how a damned soul could possibly be given such a fine home. It was located in that quarter of Hell reserved for deceased government officials, Congressmen, former dictators and the like. The garbage was picked regularly once a month, and few dogs polluted the lawns of neighbors. Probably the most unpleasant aspect was the torrent of screams of pain from the homes of Adolph Hitler and Joseph Stalin, reflecting the high level of torture inflicted on them because of their crimes on earth.

Smuthers, who had served in the United States Senate for three terms before joining being killed in a plane accident while campaigning for re-election, was very pleased by his abode. Given the fact that as a politician he had been involved in corrupt deals and was now a damned soul in Hell, his treatment was really quite good. There was only one problem. He never got to spend any time in his house. What matter than it had a very an Olympic sized swimming pool or a well manicured lawn or that its tennis court was always in perfect shape. What matter that his large household staff included a celebrity chef and a pastry cook? He never was at home to enjoy

With amazing frequency, Smuthers was dispatched by Satan around the world on missions utilizing his diplomatic skill. One day he was in deepest Africa, the next in the Middle East, the next in Latin America. A few hours after returning home from abroad, before he had a chance even to change into a clean shirt or have a hot meal, the Devil would send for him again give him another mission. And it was not as though he was able to accomplish anything on these trips. The individuals he was forced to talk with were all either simpletons too stupid to comprehend what he told them or so pompous they refused to listen to anyone but themselves.

Finally, he could stand this no more. Returning from one particularly unpleasant mission thoroughly exhausted, his stomach rebelling from the horrible that's he had been obliged to eat, his head throbbing from lack of sleep, he had gone directly to Satan's office before stopping off at his home. The Arch Fiend received him at once.

After the turbulent plane ride, Smuthers found the Devil's office pleasant, the air conditioning making this the coolest place in Hell. "What a pleasure," Satan said. Satan was seated in a comfortable desk chair behind a large desk. On the walls were several plaques testifying to the efficiency of his office. In the center there was a large photograph, showing him in the full regalia of an angel, back before he rebelled against God and was sent down to reign over Hell.

Smuthers launched into his complaints. He did not object to being sent to Hell. After all, he had been a politician and individuals entering politics must realize that they are placing their immortal souls in jeopardy. But he honestly felt that a shorter time in Hell rather than all eternity was the proper answer and that at a minimum the torture he was being subjected to was unfair and that some amelioration of his treatment.

The devil sat silently, pondering. From the time to time, he scratched his head with his tail. Finally, he spoke. Satan, of course, has no mercy within him nor tenderness, but occasionally what appear to be signs of fairness come through. This seems to be the case now.

"What you say, Mr. Smuthers," he said with a smile that might also have been a leer, "Does seem to have an element of truth in it, your treatment is definitely different from that accorded other souls in Hell. Unfortunately, my hands are tied. There is not much I can do to remedy the situation. I certainly can't discharge you from Hell and give you a pass to Heaven. Even you would have to admit that would not be justified. As for reducing your period in Hell, the administrative procedures preclude that.

The Arch Fiend fell silent. Smuthers rose to leave, defeated, when Satan spoke again. "You know," he said, "There is something I might be able to do. It rarely happens that someone is sent to Hell as a result of mechanical failure. When that happens, I can send them back to life, to give them so to speak a second chance. Naturally, your old body has been disposed of, but there are some available occasionally. Let me so what I can do."

The Devil does not always lie; sometimes he speaks the truth for his own purposes. One day after only a brief period of continued torture, Smuthers found himself back on Earth in a new body. He had just graduated from law school and was trying to decide what career path he should choose. The reborn Smuthers possessed one advantage not shared by any living person. He retained a full memory of what Hell was like and how his previous conduct and led him to end up there.

Initially, Smuthers decided to become a district attorney and devote his life to obtaining proper punishment for malefactors and protection of the innocent. In this way, he would do enough good to avoid Hell. Eventually, he concluded that an even surer means to assure a place in Heaven was for him to-become a politician again. With his special knowledge, he would be able to avoid all of the practices that had led him into Hell before. In this way, he might do more good for more people than an as district attorney.

Despite the many challenges to such a course of action,

Smuthers carried out his plan without deviation. Unlike other politicians, he never once did anything the least bit unethical or illegal. He made sure that his campaign expenses were also audited several times over to insure against accidental improprieties.. Most atypically, he never promised to deliver what he was not certain of being able to provide, regardless of how his vote would affect his popular support among the voters, he only voted for measures that would enhance the public good.

By the time Smuthers was elected to the United States Senate, he was nicknamed "Honest John" by the Washington press corps. His reputation grew to the extent that the President, seeking to re-store public confidence in the administration after a series of scan-dals, each worse than the one before, nominated him to be Secre-tary of State. Although he would damage his reputation by joining an administration so tarred by scandal, he unselfishly accepted the post in the expectation that he now might be able to help not just the citizens of the United States, but also m the oppressed popula-tions of the world.

As Secretary of state, Smuthers traveled around the globe tire-lessly, attempting to resolver international crises, to provide hu-manitarian assistance and to prevent wars and genocide. In many respects, his existence was as difficult as it and been when he was being employed by the Devil. This time, however, Smuthers knew he was advancing the cause of good, not evil and was insuring his eventual future in Heaven.

Sadly, on one such trip, Smuthers' aircraft suffered series me-chanical failure. The plane crashed into a mountain, killing every-one on board, including the Secretary of State. Smuthers regained consciousness to find himself back in Hell, in his old residence. He rushed to see the Devil to complain and was immediately ushered in to Satan's office.

The office and the Arch Fiend looked unchanged. "This is most unfair," Smuthers declared, sputtering with anger. "I did ev-erything I could to redeem myself. I shouldn't be here now. It is most, most unfair."

"Indeed it is," agreed the Devil smiling. Although the Devil is without mercy or tenderness, he is well known for having a rather unusual sense of humor.

Bancroft's Time Machine

You almost certainly have never heard of Arthur Bancroft time machine. This is because of his efforts to hide its existence. Unlike virtually every other effort to achieve this elusive goal, it was successful. Not only successful. His machine was easy to assembly and made out of easily obtainable components. He made a large number of machines for testing purposes and began the trials. This revealed only one minor defect. Although it could go forward in time to any desired period or go backward in the same fashion, his time machinery could only make a one-way trip. In short, once a person took it into the future or the past, he was stuck permanently in that period. He could not return.

It took a long time and the expenditure of many machines for Bancroft to accept the situation. In his first test of it, he set the control for an hour in the future, sent it off on its trip and waited patiently for an hour for it to reappear. To his disappointment it failed to do so. He waited another hour and then another. Finally, he concluded that he must have made an error in setting the control of the machine and tried the experiment again. The result was the same. It had gone for good.

Bancroft comforted himself with the possibility that while the mechanism to travel into the future needed some adjustment, the machine would still function properly if sent into the past. He set the controls for the machine to travel to the past, but to a slightly different site, his upstairs bedroom instead of hi laboratory. The machine vanished as before. Bancroft raced upstairs to his bedroom, hoping to find that the machine had arrived there an hour before. Once again, there was no time machine. Another failure.

Test after test produced the same result. He took the machine apart, examined each component carefully for flaws and found nothing. He reassembled the time machine and tried again, both trips to the past and to the future. Still total failure. Not a single machine every returned.

This defect was clearly a serious obstacle to its sale and use. Bancroft tried a hard as he could, but could find no solution. A lesser person would have thrown in the towel and admitted defeat. Not Arthur Bancroft. After so much hard work and coming so close to attaining his goal, Bancroft was not about to do so. He remembered what his father had told him, "If you end up in life with lemons, you can always make lemonade." Taking his father's advice to heart, he resolved to find a lucrative use for his time machine.

The effort required quite a bit if effort. After some false starts he managed to gain admittance to the office of the local crime lord, who was about to be arrested for multiple murders. Bancroft suggested that if the crime lord could somehow lure the witnesses who could testify to his guilt to Bancroft's home, he would dispose of them so that their bodies would never be discovered. Of course, the charge for this service quoted by Bancroft was a steep one, but Bancroft pointed out it was still cheaper than having to hire henchmen to do the dirty work and then to find a safe place to dump the corpses.

When he explained to the dubious crime lord his method of insuring that no witnesses would ever be seen again, the crime lord was dubious. Still he had no other alternative. After conferring with his consigliore and other top lieutenants he accepted Bancroft's terms after some hard bargaining on price which revealed the skills which had enabled him to rise to the top of his profession. Eventually, Bancroft agreed to a lot price for up to a dozen witnesses, concluding that this deal if successful would lead to healthier cash rewards in the future.

A short time later some thugs belonging to the crime lord's "family" deposited at Bancroft's home eight potential witnesses suitably bound who might have provided testimony confirming the crime lord's involvement in a large number of gang-land murders. Each one was carefully placed in one of Bancroft's time machines and dispatched into the far future, none less than ninety years ahead and arriving at ten year intervals. As Bancroft had carefully explained to the crime lord, a ninety year period should be sufficient for the crime lord to have gone on to his future reward.

Bancroft felt queasy about participating in such an activity. He comforted himself with the knowledge that these potential witnesses would have been murdered without his involvement and that life in the future, no matter how unpleasant, was preferable to their meeting a quick and violent death. Bancroft's effort to reassure himself of the relatively high moral tone of his actions, all things considered, was once again strained. The crime lord arrived unexpectedly after the witnesses had been sent off and unexpectedly shoot the underlings who had brought the witnesses to Bancroft. He explained that it was better not to leave loose ends and that it would be foolish of him to eliminate one set of potentially life-threatening witnesses only to create a new potential threat.

Then the crime lord added to Bancroft's alarm by insisting that he disposing of his late henchmen in the same manner and for the same original price he had handled the witnesses, Bancroft prudently interpreted this to be an off he couldn't refuse. He agreed, but politely observed that he was losing money on the deal if his depreciation costs were added in and that he could continue to provide the service only if the volume of his business expanded. He also suggested that if the crime lord was interested in becoming a partner, he could take fifty percent of the purchase price from any new business he could steer to Bancroft.

The crime lord gladly accepted Bancroft's proposal and added that if Bancroft had been of Sicilian extraction he would have been proud to endorse Bancroft's becoming a member of the Mafia. Thanks to the crime boss's help, Bancroft's business grew rapidly. He no longer attempted to correct what he had previously considered a flaw in the time machine, its inability to make a return trip. He instead spent all of his time constructing more machines to handle the increased level of disposals.

Because secrecy of his operation was essential, Bancroft had to do all of the work himself. He also did not register his time machine at the patent office or publicize its invention in scientific journals, as he had once planned to do. Given popular skepticism if the possibility of time travels he did not fear that any new research was being conducted in the area.

At the end of two years, Bancroft was servicing all of the major crime syndicates east of the Mississippi and he was contemplating expanding operations into Nevada and California. Thanks to his hefty returns, he now dressed only in five hundred dollar suits. He lived in a luxurious mansion on New York's Park Avenue. Summers Bancroft vacationed at his compound on Cape Cod adjacent to that of the Kennedy family and he spent several weeks each winter in his Palm Beach Florida retreat. He has never married for fear of a wife learning the details of his work, but he is always surrounded by a bevy of beautiful and very willing women.

Today, thanks to his invention, Bancroft is a very happy and very wealthy man. He has long since abandoned the dreams he had of fame and of winning the Nobel Prize in Physics for his invention. He is content to have settled for wealth and comfort. He readily admits, if you ask him, that he owes all to his acting on his father's advice, "If you end up with lemons, make lemonade."

The Enemies Machine

The multi-million dollar super computer dubbed the "Enemies Machine" was constructed under the direction of the Advanced Research Project Agency under the overall supervision of senior Pentagon officials. Once built, the CIA and other members of the Intelligence Community played the major role in providing data to be inputted into it. It belonged to the first generation that can properly be said to think. Much like the human brain, its circuits were wired so that rather than just being limited to pulling up individual pieces of data, it was able on its own to recombine them in every possible combination and then provide the most logical answers to the questions asked of it.

The project was started on the orders of some of Washington's top policy makers. The members of the President's National Security Council believed they were handicapped in dealing with various word crises by the incorrect advice they were receiving from the intelligence community. Intelligence analysts, even those with the deepest knowledge of a foreign country, tended to base their predilections on what that nation's response to U.S. moves might be to their own view of the universe. In other words, they were unable to view anything from the perspective of the foreign leaders. While this admittedly reflected a good deal of Monday morning quarterbacking, the President believed the "Enemies Machine" would provide a useful adjunct to the existing National Security Council apparatus and authorized expenditure of the required funds.

The "Enemies Machine" was seen as providing the solution. Into its data banks were imputed all of the many separate items of information bearing upon the geography, history, culture, society, economy, political structure and religion of the various countries. Because of the then limited capacity of the computer, not every nation in the world could be included. Therefore, the database was limited to only the ten nations considered most likely to be involved in a serious world crisis affecting the U.D. These included Russia, China, North Korea, Cuba, Iran, Saudi Arabia, Afghanistan and Iran. In the light of later events, the most significant omissions were Syria and Venezuela. Another shortcoming was the failure to consider Ukraine as a nation separate from Russia.

To enhance the accuracy of its estimates, the machine was given a brilliantly designed internal map projection capability, so that its responses were based on the geo-strategic viewpoint that would be those of the host populations and their leaders. Since in virtually every country of the world maps prepared in that country show it as the center of the world, this was the underpinning for the machine's analysis.

The first test of the computer was and after the fact re-examination of the probable Iranian reaction to the ouster of Iranian Prime Minister Mohammad Mossadegh in a coup involving the United States. It correctly predicted the popular furor caused by the overthrow of the democratically elected leader and the likely build up of a violently anti-American sentiment. This analysis so pleased the president that he ordered henceforth U.S. actions in any world crisis be based on the readout from the "Enemies Machine."

The first test of the machine in real-time came when American policymakers considered re-orienting the thrust of U.S. policy away from Europe and the Middle East to give the situation in the Far East the highest priority. When the machine was asked to provide the probable response to the so-called "pivot" in policy, it responded with a prediction that the Chinese Communist Government would interpret the move as a deliberate American provocation revealing a hostile intent in Washington. No American offer of increased military cooperation with China or public expression of good will would convince Beijing otherwise.

Shortly thereafter, the pro-Russian President of Ukraine Viktor Yamukovych was forced from power by public demonstrations in Kiev by agitators favoring close association of the country with the European Community, the "Enemies Machine" was asked to provide analysis of the probable Russian reaction. The answer was that Russian President Putin would never accept this as fait accompli but would resort to whatever tactics required to keep Ukraine from slipping out of the Russian economic orbit. Neither Western promises of continued good will toward Russia nor threats of economic sanctions would induce the Russian President to abandon his goal.

These analyses were submitted to the National Security Council, which did not know what to do. If accepted as accurate predictions, they would require a significant change in the direction of American foreign policy. Could or should Washington abandon its traditional goal for every U.S. foreign policy initiative? How could the Washington political establishment countenance abandoning its firm belief that the establishment of popular democracy in every nation of the world, regardless of the level of education, standard of living, hostile attitude toward the U.S. or religious fanaticism deserved the highest priority for the long term, regardless of the scope of unfavorable results in the short and medium term?

The problem was deemed too important for the National Security Council to decide, and so it was taken directly to the president. The Chief Executive weighed the issue carefully, carefully considering all aspects. Then he made his decision. The traditional all-out drive for global world democracy could not be reversed nor even modified in the smallest degree. He ordered that all documents referring in any way to the recommendations of the "Enemies Machine" be shredded and burned. To prevent any future re-occurrence of such obviously unsound estimated, he decreed that the machine be destroyed along with all documents relating to its design or use.

Today, the citizens of the United States and indeed of the entire world can rest easier in their homes. They know that no considerations of national self-interest or of common sense will be permitted to intrude into American foreign policy.

Eat Up No More

Senator Homer Bigger rose to the position of second ranking majority member of the Senate Foreign Relations Committee, despite the fact that he had no knowledge and cared less about international affairs. His assignment by the Senate Majority Leader to the prestigious committee had been the result of his having two useful personality traits; he was so placid he was frequently described as "inert", and he could be relied upon to say or do anything the Majority Leader suggested.

The Senator was justly proud about his appointment to the prestigious committee. Similarly, the Majority Leader was proud of his ability to find the perfect person for the job. In the recent off-year election, the President's party had suffered heavy losses in the senatorial voting. As a result, it now held only a one vote majority among the ninety-nine Senators who could be counted upon to attend Senate sessions. The senior Senator from Mississippi had been in a coma for the previous fourteen months and with no replacement picked to date. The Mississippi Governor was reluctant to pick a successor because of the probable controversy that would result. Thus, the Committee vote was always nine to eight, with Senator Bigger casting the decisive ninth vote for the majority.

Normally, international affairs play a secondary role in Washington's political controversies, well behind domestic affairs. The results of the off-year elections, however, meant that the President would find it impossible to push any significant domestic legislation through the sharply divided Senate. The only alternative, if he was to establish his place in history, was to turn to the area of international affairs. The President directed his advisers to produce a dramatic new initiative, and after intense deliberation they succeeded. Stressing the vital necessity to fill alleged glaring gaps in the nation's security defenses, the President utilized his State of the Union speech as the platform from which to launch the East European Treaty Union for Peace.

A major advantage of the new doctrine, which was linked in the press with the President's name, was its acronym, EAT UP. Focus groups universally gave the doctrine a favorable response, as long as it was coupled with EAT UP, a reaction explained by some editorial writers as reflecting the subliminal craving of most Americans for more food. Hearings by the Senate Foreign relations proceeded with no significant opposition voiced against the proposed treaty, which would bind the United States to come to the aid of the East European nations, including those not members of NATO, if they were subjected to attack.

The day of the final committee vote on EAT UP came, with all Washington expecting it would pass by the customary eight to seven vote. Surprisingly, the committee room was packed, most unlike the custom at most such hearings. The reason, unknown to the Senators, is that most of the people in the committee room were time travelers, who had come from the future to view this event, so critical in the history of the world. They were all aware from their history books, although the Senators could not have known that the passage of Eat Up would be cited by future historians as the most important single event leading up to the First Atomic War.

The vote on the treaty was called, and the tally stood at eight to eight, as Senator Bigger was about to cast the deciding ninth vote in favor. Suddenly, looking at the Chairman, Bigger saw a giant spider descending by a threat, about to land on the Chairman's bald head. Bigger couldn't stop himself. The Senator harbored a horror of spiders. Without thinking he shouted "No! Good God, No!" at the top of his lungs.

The recorder, hearing Bigger, recorded him as voting against the treaty and announced the proposal had been rejected. Startled, the Chairman dropped his gavel. The reaction among the onlookers was even more dramatic. The time travelers stared at each with amazement and debated what had happened in loud tones... How could this happen? Could their history books be all wrong?

Normally, the error would have been rectified. Senator Bigger could have changed his vote, thereby passing EAT UP. However, Bigger's apparent negative vote produced an interesting reaction in the junior Senator from Massachusetts, the most recent appointee to the committee after Bigger. Although a member of the majority party, he knew that public opinion in his state was strongly against the treaty and that his vote in favor might well cost him his seat in the next election. Feeling protected by Senator Bigger's negative vote, he quickly changed his vote to negative as well. With the EAT UP treaty defeated by two votes it was dead, as dead as a door nail.

Neither Senator Bigger nor any of his colleagues nor the general public has ever learned by what a narrow margin the world escaped the threat of nuclear holocaust. As we contemplate this, it may also be instructive to think of what kind of world faced the time travelers who had been in the Committee Room as they rushed back to the future, eager to learn how history may have been changed.

The Devil You Know

Count Ernst Frederick von Brautisch sat in the drawing room of his castle. The vast chamber was illuminated by a single flickering torch, which cast a dim light. It was very cold in the room, and the count wrapped his cloak about him in a vain effort to keep warm. He wished that he had enough money to buy coal or charcoal to use in the fireplace. Despite his vast estates, his lineage and the regard with which he was held by the other officers in his regiment, he was essentially penniless. His grandfather and then his father had both dissipated most of the family wealth through gambling excessively. The count, a frugal man, had attempted to preserve his very limited inheritance. However, there had been too many obligatory expenses for him to come even close to living up to the life style expected of an army officer.

The count was sitting behind a large mahogany desk, his hand resting on the open desk drawer. He could just see within it his revolver. All he had to do was to fire it once into his temple, and all his troubles would be over. It was the only alternative left. He wondered if he should write a suicide note, but decided that would be foolish. There was no one he wished to say goodbye to. Fortunately, he had never married and so there was no wife or children who would be saddened by his departure. He took out the revolver and placed it against his temple. His finger tightened against the trigger.

Suddenly there was a brilliant flash of light in the fireplace. Flames licked out from it, and a small figure emerged. It was about three and a half feet tall and approximated human shape. A little horn protruded from each side of its head, and it had a small tail. "Are you Count von Brautisch?" it asked in a surprisingly deep voice.

The count was so shaken that he dropped his revolver, which fell to the floor. There was a sharp crack as it fired, the bullet, fortunately, imbedding itself in the wall rather than hitting the count. "I am Count Ernst Frederick von Brautisch" he managed to answer.

"Permit me to introduce myself," the thing from the fireplace said. My name is Astaroth."

He shook himself daintily, some ashes falling off him.

"Are you the Devil?" the Count asked. "Have you come to offer me something in exchange for my soul?"

"Oh, no," Astaroth replied. "I'm one of his assistants."

So you don't want my soul?" von Brautisch was somewhat disappointed. After all, his soul wasn't doing him any particular good right now and trading it off for something useful like great wealth would have solved his immediate predicament.

"Only my boss can barter for souls," the demon explained. "Actually, I'm here on personal business."

The count's innate politeness came into play. He was after all the host. He would have offered Astaroth a drink if he had any in the castle.

What can I do for you?" he asked.

"A mere trifle I assume you are still unmarried."

"I am."

"Good," said the demon. "My sister has been nagging me incessantly to find a husband for my nice, Brunhilda. The girl is determined to marry a nobleman. You would be the perfect match for her."

"And in return for marrying your niece," the count said, "You will grant me great wealth."

"Don't be foolish," Astaroth answered. "Only the boss can do that."

"Well, just what are you offering in exchange?"

"I'm certain," the demon answered, that I can persuade your bankers in Florence to refinance the mortgage on your castle. With a longer period for paying it off, you would be able to reduce your annual payments to a quarter of your military pay, which should end your worries about losing your castle.'

"That's preposterous! The count exclaimed. Take on your niece as my wife for only a loan rescheduling!"

Astaroth shrugged. He took out a long list from one of the folds of his body and examined it. "There are quite a few impoverished noblemen; I dare say, who will accept my offer."

The count reconsidered. "All right," he said, "Let me take a look at Brunhilda. If she's not too bad looking, I may accept your offer.

"That's a reasonable position," the demon said. He returned to the fireplace and disappeared. A few seconds later there was another flash of flames in the fireplace and Astaroth emerged, followed by a young woman. She was taller than Astaroth, but still quite tiny. Her hair was piled up on her head, covering up any horns she might have had. All in all, she was a relatively attractive young woman.

"All right," said von Brautisch, "I'll marry her."

"Thank you, Count," Brunhilda said. "I'll be the perfect wife for you."

"You realize," the count said, looking at them both, "That I don't have any funds to pay for the wedding. I don't even have enough to give to the clergyman who performs the ceremony."

Astaroth looked shocked, and he crossed himself backwards. "God damn it! He exclaimed, "If I may be forgiven for using that expression. We will have to have a civil ceremony, nothing religious!"

And so it was. The only guest at the wedding was von Brautisch's orderly, who doubled as best man. The count found himself pleased with his wife as the months passed. She was frugal, helping him to lower his expenses and turned out to be an astonishingly good cook. Even more important, she was fabulous in bed. The colonel of von Brautisch's regiment, upon meeting Brunhilda, was taken by her charm. He assured the count that with a wife like that to help him, he could not fail to become a general.

The count prudently did not attempt to determine whether Brunhilda was a demon or a human. She always refused to disrobe and get into bed unless the bedroom was completely dark. Von Brautisch always remembered during their love making not to caress her too far down the back to where a tail, if she had one, would be.

Unfortunately after several years of married bliss, disaster struck. Von Brautish found himself unable to refuse the invitation of three of his brother officers to accompany them to a local tavern. They all drank far more than they should have as they exchanged ribald jokes and stared lasciviously at the entertainer, the most voluptuous woman von Brautish had ever seen. When she took a break in her singing, one of the officers invited her to join them at their table.

At the table, the woman surprisingly concentrated her attentions on the count, ignoring the other three officers. She stared into his eyes, licking her crimson lips with a lewd smile. As she leaned towards him, her low cut costume appeared to slip, revealing virtually all of her bosom. Then von Brautisch felt her hand on his thigh, squeezing it.

The count was far from being a ladies' man, and he sincerely wished to be faithful to his wife, but he had drunk too much to have a clear head. Then one of his brother officers stood up and declared in a loud voice that he had to return to his quarters as he had duty tomorrow. A second of von Brautisch's comrades did the same. Wobbling and trying clumsily to help each other, they headed for the door. The count looked at the third officer. He was slumped down, his head on the table, snoring loudly.

"Come, Ernst," said the woman, addressing him by his given name. "Why don't we go up to my room? We will be much more comfortable there." He struggled to stand and then managed to walk, following her up the stairs to her room.

Lorelei, as she had identified herself to the count, turned and faced him. He thought she was even more voluptuous woman than she had seemed downstairs and desired to possess her with every pore of his body. Slowly, seductively, she lowered the light in the bedroom, until the count could barely see her figure, illuminated by a bit of moonlight, streaming in through the window. Then she removed her costume with a single gesture and stood there naked facing him.

The count ripped off her clothes and pushed her down upon the bed, then climbed atop her. Pressing himself against her, he experienced the most wonderful sex he had ever knowb1n. She bit him hard upon the lips, which only excited him more. His hands caressed her body until, to his sudden shock; he felt a furry tail. Then she bit him savagely on the neck, breaking it.

The last conscious thought von Brautisch had before he expired was of some advice his father had given him, so many years ago. "My son," he had said, "Always take care. Remember, the devil you know is far better than the devil you don't."

The Vulcan Project

The possibility of some form of life existing in the center of the earth has been the subject of occasional science fiction stories but until recently was not an area of series scientific exploration. This gap or supposed gap in human knowledge was closed by the inauguration of the Vulcan Project. The concept originated in the mind of Senator Nettles, widely considered to be the most influential member of the U.S. Senate. Nettles was not in the least interested in scientific research. His motivation came from the unhappy situation in his statement, which was suffering from the highest unemployment rate in the country due to the closure of many mines coinciding with the upcoming Congressional elections. No political observer could be found with the temerity that the Senator might possibly be re-elected.

Nettles at first tried to pursue the standard remedies. However, government social welfare had lost the public's support because of their total lack of success. As a result, he made no headway when he tried to increase the time the residents of his state would be eligible for unemployment insurance or to obtain government-financed retraining. The Vulcan Project, as he conceived it, met the need perfectly. He proposed to spend a trillion dollars over a ten-year period to finance the digging of a giant hole to the center of the earth to determine whether there was any life form there. Since it was a government project, the total lack of any rational element in the project was of no importance.

Naturally, the mouth of the hole would be situated in Nettles' home state, which was justified on the basis of the many experienced miners living there. Even if the project had some scientific purpose, a hole with a diameter of say three feet would have been more than adequate. However, such a tunnel would have appeared to be a mere pinprick, totally insufficient for publicity purposes. Therefore, it was to be a round hundred feet in diameter, or more than twice the size of the widest tunnel in the world, that under the Yangzi River in China.

As powerful as he was, Senator Nettles alone could not assure Senatorial passage of his Vulcan Project bill. Looking at possible allies, he selected Senator Cooper, another powerful member of that body. Like Nettles, Cooper had not the least interest in promoting scientific research. However, his home state was the site of numerous plants involved in the automobile manufacture. Declining American car sales and the steady rise in production costs and wages had pushed virtually all of these firms close to bankruptcy, many for the third time in the previous five years. C

Copper readily agreed to back the Vulcan bill, provided it was amended to include a few minor provisions. These all boiled down to the bailing out of the auto companies in his state. Since previous such bailouts had aroused bitter attacks of unfairness from those parties not included in the bailout, the provisions of the new bill were slightly altered. Not just workers' pensions, but also workers' wages, bond holders, senior executives and stock owners were all guaranteed against financial loss. The bill for this was a comparatively modest four hundred billion dollars, which was added to the original one trillion dollar proposal.

With Cooper's support, passage of the plan was virtually assured. However, Nettles was not in the mood to gamble. Fortunately, Senator Zeiss offered voluntarily to deliver his support. Unlike Nettles and Cooper, Zeiss was one of the few members of the

Senate to actually consider what might be beneficial for the entire country.

Zeiss was the only member of the Senate to hold a Ph.D. degree, which was in the field of chemistry. He was passionately motivated to improve scientific research in the U.S., which he felt was suffering as a result of most students concluding that neither graduate school nor a basic college education paid off financially in view of the difficulty in obtaining suitable jobs after graduation. Indeed, all but a handful of graduates were forced to take minimum wage job in the fast food industry or in the fast growing hallucinogenic drug retail business.

With Zeiss expressing great gratification, the Vulcan Project bill was further amended to include an additional two hundred billion dollars.Half of the added amount was to go in fellowships to worthy students in biology, chemistry, physics and engineering and the other half in grants to schools around the country to finance expansion of their facilities for scientific education and research. The final version of the bill now financed at three trillion, four hundred million dollars over ten years passed the Senate with an overriding majority and then sailed through the House of Representatives. The path to approval was smoothed by the Chairman of the Federal Reserve System. He endorsed the Vulcan bill. In return he obtained the commitment by Senators and Cooper to free him from the requirement to appear periodically before Congressional Committees to testify on the actions of the Federal Reserve and on economic conditions in general.

The President, far from opposing the plan, warmly endorsed it and then claimed full credit for the idea. His popularity in the public opinion polls had fallen to such a low level that he now spent over three hundred days each year playing golf in the hinterland to avoid the unpleasant reminders in Washington of his ineptitude. His impact on the public matters was now so minimal that even the Sunday morning TV network news shows turned down out of hand his pleadings to appear as their guest.

Having no accomplishments of which to boast, at the State of the Union Message to Congress he blatantly declared that the Vulcan Project was the most important U.S. Government program since President Kennedy's launching in March 1961 of the program to land a man on the moon. Attempting to duplicating the fine Kennedy rhetoric, the President declared that "Just as this country became the first nation to place a man on the moon, we will be the first nation to place a man in the center of the earth."

The speed with which work on the Vulcan project began reflected the crescendo of support from all political factions in Congress which followed the President's State of the Union Speech. First priority went to the construction of a large media center at the planned site of the excavation in view of the urgency of assuring favorable media coverage of the project. No expense was spared. The complete included two Olympic sized swimming pools, a complete motion picture theater and an eighteen hole golf course. Three separate restaurants, each directed by a celebrity chef, supplied meals to the media representatives, all without charge. Due to various government regulations, free liquor could not be served, but lengthy "happy hours" which lasted for most of each day saw alcoholic beverages sold for a token price which as further cut on Mondays, Wednesdays and Fridays.

To ensure that the facility was readily available to the media, free government air transportation was provided to it from all major cities. In the center auditorium, media representatives were given informative briefings on the state of the project, with considerable free time for them to prepare their news stories and also to enjoy the many amenities such as the golf course. Because of the press of demand, most stays at the center had to be limited to no more than three weeks, particularly when the media representatives were accompanied by their spouses and children.

Following the completion of the media center, the next structure constructed was Mission Control. This facility was the home for several hundred scientists and researchers who sat at large mahogany desks studying computer screens and a wide variety of gauges and graphic displays. These graphic displays were designed with priority assigned to providing interesting video footage when they were shown on TV programs. The actual data provided by them had nothing at all to do with the actual project, measuring developments which had no bearing at all on the project such as the weather in Greenland or the daily tidal range in Portland, Maine.

After these most important features had been taken care of, work on the actual excavation began. Day after day, week after week and year after year the digging went on. After each twenty feet were dug, the announcement of this feat was made at a giant press conference in the media center. Frequently the President or the Vice President would take the occasion to deliver a televised speech. When the first ten-year period, financing for a second ten year period was passed with little struggle.

Everyone concerned was happy about the project. Senator Nettles easily won re-election and served an additional two terms before retiring to take a highly paid job as a lobbyist in Washington. Senator Cooper was similarly pleased by the renewed financial strength given by the bailout to the auto industry companies in his state, which kept them out of bankruptcy for at least another three years. Of the three principal Senatorial backers of the plan, only Senator Zeiss was somewhat disappointed by the results. Although the funds promised under the legislation for fellowships funding of scientific education and research were provided as promised, American scientific prowess did not stop or even slow its rapid decline. The funds provided were still insufficient to redress the balance between what students had to expend in on postsecondary school education with the difficulty to obtaining adequately paid jobs after graduation. In actuality, the great majority of the money actually went to providing for improved facilities for the faculty, particularly faculty dining rooms and tennis courts.

Scientific research and education were spent, American scientific prowess.

Eventually, this happy state was cruelly shattered when the excavation reached the center of the earth, with no signs of life discovered there. Alarm rose throughout the country that the project might be ended, with no further funding. All of the groups in society that had benefitted from the massive government spending provided by the project feared that the gravy train had ended. To deal with the problem, the President took the traditional presidential approach to dealing with such a problem. He named a blue ribbon commission to look into it and to recommend the proper policy to pursue.

As was the case followed in the creation of such commissions, all of the proposed members were carefully vetted before appointment to determine their views on the matter. It was, therefore, a foregone conclusion when the body submitted its final report and recommendations. The original purpose and implementation of the Vulcan Project had been worthy of commendation. The inability to uncover any life form in the center of the earth was simply due to an understandable error in the selection of the site for excavation. This time, two rather than one excavation project was the proper choice to ensure greater coverage of the core of the earth's core.

Congress immediately approved the continuation of Vulcan Project to the tune of six trillion four hundred billion dollars over the next ten year period. In the interests of economy, the sponsors noted that the amount to be appropriated for a bailout of the auto industry plants and funding the scientific research and education area had been left unchanged, ignoring despite the high annual rate of inflation. Two new states were chosen as the sites for the project. Each one was a state which had benefitted from rapid population growth since the original project was established and which now benefitted from exercising much larger political power in the national elections and in the House of Representatives.

The renewal of Project Vulcan stimulated increased concern over how to dispose of the immense quantity of fill generated by

the project. During the early decades, all of the possible fill dispos-
al sites on land had reached and then surpassed acceptable limits.
It then had become necessary of dispose of the fill as is done with
most of the world's refuse by dumping it into the Atlantic Ocean.
The fill now generated from two excavations resulted in the Atlantic Ocean being completely filled in. The land bridge thus created
connecting Africa with the United States. Most of the population
of Africa trudged across it to seek political asylum in the U.S., a
movement encouraged by the recent Congressional legislation re-
quiring that refugee status be extended to anyone in the World
injured by having a standard of living lower than the average prevailing in this country.

All was going well when fate intervened. The covering up, of
the Atlantic Ocean, the massive amounts of fill now being dumped
into the Pacific Ocean and the t funneling out of so much of the
Earth's interior caused the Earth to begin to wobble on its orbit
around the sun. As the orbit became increasingly erratic, the Earth
moved too far and collided with the planet Venus, causing both of
them to shatter into fragments, the biggest pieces of which were
attracted by gravitational pull of the largest plant, Jupiter, and now
revolve around it as additional moons. The planet closest to the
Sun, losing the gravitational pull formerly exercised by Earth and
Venus, fell into the Sun and vanished in a brief solar flare-up.

The destruction of the Earth, Venus and Mercury were observed by astronomers on the planet Broma Three, the planet
closest to the Solar system having an intelligent life form. Since
because of the vast distance it had taken eons for the light of the
catastrophe to reach observers on Broma Three, it was far too late
for them to do anything about it, even if they had wished to do
so. It is highly unlikely that any of the historians on Broma Three
knew about the details of Vulcan Project to render an informed
judgment concerning the wisdom of the endeavor. However, they
might have benefitted from the conviction in the United States immediately before the destruction of the Earth than Project Vulcan

was by far the most thoughtful and best executed program ever implemented by the federal government.

Obesity

Conditions in the United States and the rest of the developed world were deteriorating so rapidly that there could be no overlooking the problem. The President summoned an emergency session of the National Security Council and instructed them to come with a solution. For several days, they met and hotly debated the probable causes and how to remedy the situation. Realizing that the situation was so dire that they had to do something, they finally agreed to call in Dr. Kroutmier. The doctor was probably the most important unofficial adviser the government had ever had. A professor at the Cambridge School of Advanced Strategic Studies, he was widely regarded as a combination of Henry Kissinger and Bernard Baruch.

As usual, Dr. Kroutmier's schedule was fully booked for several months ahead, but he graciously agreed to travel to Washington and meet with the National Security Council the next weekend. The president's senior advisers gathered in their high-security conference room, eagerly awaiting the doctor's council. He Stroud in so purposefully that it was apparent to all that his was the dominant personality in the room. He demanded a slide projector, ordered the room lights to be dimmed, and with an attitude much like that of a teacher instructing dull students, turned on the projector.

On the screen appeared a chart with two curves, one in green and one in red. The green line began very high on the vertical axis of the chart and plunged downward to the horizontal axes. The red line behaved in the reverse fashion, starting off low and climbing sharply. The red curve, the doctor, explained represented the rise in the problems of the United States. The green curve represented the calorie intake of the average American. There is not the slightest doubt; Kupatsky declared, that the decline of the U.S. position in the world was due to the popular movement in this country to adopt a more healthy diet.

His listeners sat astounded. Many thought he had suddenly lost his wits. Others concluded that they had misunderstood him because of his strong German accent. The Secretary of Defense went so far as to utter a crude epithet and get up in disgust. Fortunately, a junior staff aide who had been ordered to the meeting to act as recorder suggested that they might submit the doctor's theory to the secret government giant computer. It was a convenient face-saving exercise. The National Security Council voted unanimously to take this action and hastily left the conference room.

Much to everyone's surprise, the giant computer confirmed Dr. Kroutmier's analysis. The National Security Council convened again and unanimously concluded that the computer had somehow malfunctioned. The doctor's theory was just too absurd to be possible. Confident that another computer would dispel the nonsense, they sent the readout of the giant computer to a still bigger computer used by the National Weather Bureau to forecast the daily weather for the next century.

The National Weather Service was reluctant to permit their computer to be diverted to mundane issues but agreed when the President personally ordered them to do so. Once again, Kupatsky's theory was confirmed. There could be no doubt. The proximate cause for the decline of the U.S. and its allies was the fall in average caloric consumption.

There was no time to lose. In the interests of speed, the President used his executive powers to order an immediate tripling of the caloric composition of the school lunch program. Fruits, vegetables and salads were all removed, to be replaced with candy, fried potatoes and soda, to which extra sugar had been added. Senior officials from the broadcast media were summoned to Camp David. There, they were informed by the President, in the company of the majority and minority party leaders of both branches of Congress, that their broadcast licenses would be voided if they did not eliminate all slender actors from their shows and replace them with obese ones. Restaurants, particularly fast food chains received subtle but nonetheless clear cut warning from the government that they would far more difficulties in their operations if they did not eliminate all healthy choices from their menus and increase the high-carb, fatty selections. Food production companies followed suite and at each stage of the manufacturing process, greatly increased amounts of salt and sugar were added.

Not surprisingly, the alarming decline in the average American's daily caloric intake stopped falling and began to rise sharply. Considering the scope of the national change in diet, a surprisingly large number of individuals remained ignorant of what was happening. The government encouraged this reaction, as did business groups. Clothing sizes were adjusted, so that the same size forty suits for men Was now the equivalent of what a size forty-four would have been previously. Both old and new customers at diet clubs found the caloric goals and weight guides set for them were not only not lower that what they had been but in fact considerably elevated. Where exercise clubs found it impossible to discourage customers from using their machines to lose weight, they were furnished and encouraged to consume so-called "health drinks" which were laced with calories and stimulants designed to increase their appetites.

In the face of such a massive campaign, which, in fact, could not be differentiated from the braining washing techniques developed by the former Communist security services of Eastern Europe, it is not surprising that it proved extremely effective. At the end of three years, the government officials administering the program submitted the data to the secret giant computer for analysis. The computer readout confirmed what had seemed obvious; problems in the United States and the rest of the developed world were on a sharply declining path with the trajectory of the rate of caloric consumption rising by the same multiple. Regrettably, a similar analysis could not be performed at the end of five years because the greatly increased girth of the technicians manning the computer now too great for them to get close enough to operate it.

All told, Professor Kroutmier's analysis of the problem, the solution he provided, and the government implementation of it may be deemed the most effective ever to come from the American government. There was only one small problem. As mankind not more and more obese, it became more and more difficult for anyone to actually work. At the same time as people demanded ever high intakes of food, farmers stopped going into the fields to produce it. Remedies might have been sought, but the fact that most people now telecommuted from their homes rather than actually producing any real work masked the problem. Mankind gradually became extinct, paralleling the fate of the carrier pigeon, the dodo and the dinosaur. When rats took over as the dominant life form on earth, they profited from what had happened to man. Search where you will, in every social stratum, and no where will you find an obese rate.

The Seers

Captain Winston Carpenter was flying his Army Air Corps plane over New Guinea in April 1944 when it developed engine failure and crashed. Because of bad flying weather, the search for survivors had to be postponed for twenty-four hours. When it was conducted, no trace of any wreckage could be spotted because of the dense foliage in many parts of New Guinea. After an appropriate period of time, Carpenter's family was formally notified that he was missing in action and had to be presumed dead.

More than fifty years passed. Then Carpenter's son, Winston Carpenter Jr., pressed the Pentagon for further information concerning his father's fate. The request would have received a routine reply except for the fact that the son was not only a member of Congress, but more importantly the second ranking member of the House Armed Services Committee. As head of one of the committee's subcommittees, he could very easily reduce or even eliminate financing for some of the proposed new weapons systems most desired by the Pentagon.

As a result of these special circumstances, the Defense Department decided to would only be fair to reopen the investigation into Captain Carpenter's fate. New reconnaissance missions were flown using the more sophisticated sensors developed since 1944. The result was the same. The dense foliage in the area prevented any thorough search airplane debris that might have been left on the ground by a crash. Given the high priority Attached to keeping Congressman Carpenter's good will, it was decided that further efforts were warranted.

One of the service secretaries recalled that the Defense Advanced Research Projects Agency had just terminated a project involved the use of seers, individuals believed to have telepathic powers to locate objects in areas in which aerial observation was not possible. Use of the seers to satisfy Congressman Carpenter's request was approved at the highest Pentagon level, and three of the most highly regarded seers were summoned back to Washington to participate. They were briefed on all the known details concerning the disappearance and probable crash of Captain Carpenter's aircraft and then placed in a room in the bowels of the Pentagon.

Seven hours later they emerged with their joint conclusion. They believed his plane had crashed in a remote area of New Guinea and furnished the map coordinates that they thought indicated the probable site. Other aerial reconnaissance missions to overfly the location were ordered. Again, the dense jungle foliage prevented any confirmation.

So great was the Pentagon's desire to retain Congressman Carpenter's good will that further efforts were ordered. The State Department obtained permission from the New Guinea authorities for an American search party to travel to the suspected crash site on foot. A search party of some dozen individuals was carefully selected. In addition to the remains identification experts, there was added a team of Navy Seals to provide security from possibly hostile indigenous tribes. The party was flown in by helicopter to the closest suitable drop-off area, and the search party then cut its way through the dense jungle.

After three days of hard going, the searchers reached the coordinates given by the seers as the probable crash site. There to their joy, the found the wreckage of an airplane that had crashed many years before. Initial joy turned to disappointment as they carefully screened the wreckage, and it became obvious that the crashed plane had not been Captain Carpenter's but of a Lockheed Electra and that Human remains in the wreckage were those of a woman of about forty years of age. The mystery was solved when some personal effects showed the pilot to have been famed aviator Amelia Earhart, who disappeared in July 1937 in the South Pacific while on a flight to circumnavigate the world.

When the search party returned to Washington, the results of the mission were interpreted as proving the utility of the seers' research. All that was needed was to improve the accuracy of the map coordinates they provided. The seers were recalled to Washington and asked to repeat the effort. Again after some hours they jointly came up with new coordinates for the probable crash site of Captain Carpenter's plane which was in the same general area as the first site they had provided. Rather than going through the time-consuming process to obtain permission authorities for the search party to again go on foot to the crash site, the Pentagon decided to just assume that the initial permission had been sufficiently broad to cover future attempts.

The search party, with most of its original members, again traveled by helicopter to the landing site in New Guinea. This time, the party had to spend four days cutting through the jungle. Once again, they were overjoyed to see a crashed airship hidden from above by the dense foliage. But it quickly became clear that the wreckage could not be the remains of Captain Carpenter's aircraft. The airship had clearly been extremely large and circular in shape. The search party approached it and saw a door in one side of the ship. Dr. Foster, the team leader, instructed the other members to stay behind and walked up to the door; He tried it, and the door swung open easily.

As he entered, and the door closed automatically behind him, some form of indirect lighting eliminated the interior. To his amazement, Foster beheld the remains of the crew. Four skeletons were found, humanoid, but clearly not those of humans. The saucer-like craft had been piloted by beings that were about three feet in height.

Foster stood there gaping, wondering what to do. He had a pretty good idea but decided to confer with his subordinates. Returning to the door, he opened it and summoned in his two senior deputies, the commander of the Seals detachment and the senior remains specialist. Ushering them into the ship, he pointed to the mains of the crew and indicated his belief that they came from outer space and that from the condition of the remains and of the wreckage he estimated that the craft had crashed here more than three centuries ago.

His colleagues agreed with Dr. Foster's conclusions. They now had to decide on the proper course to follow. The team leader noted that if news of the discovery were ever made public, it would have an incalculable effect on the religious, scientific, economic and political beliefs of the world. He added that there appeared to be no urgency in disseminating the news. After all, the wreckage had been there undetected for about five centuries without any known effects on the world. Presumably, the race that sent it might well wait another five centuries or more before taking any further action which might make their existence known to the Earth's population.

After some discussion, they all agreed on the need for extreme secrecy. They would not communicate to the other team members what they had found no transmit the news back to Washington. They further agreed to Dr. Foster's proposal, although only after some objections raised by the senior human remains specialist to completely destroy the wreckage by detonating a thermite bomb.

One by one they left the ship, Dr. Foster being the last. He told the other team members that the wreckage appeared to be that of a secret Air Force Flying Saucer experimental observation craft. It would be necessary to destroy it completely; he added, to prevent the technology from being stolen by foreign powers. The Seals leader returned to the ship, placed the thermite bomb within, set the fuse and quickly left. From a spot in the clearing far enough from the wreckage to be safe, they watched the ship explode in a cloud of smoke. When the debris lifted, Foster breathed a sigh of relief. Everything that might have suggested that the wreckage had come from outer space had vanished with the explosion.

The team sent back a curt message saying only that the wreckage had been carefully inspected and that it had been determined it definitely was not that from Captain Carpenter's missing plane. The search party then cut its way back to the helicopter pickup point and was retrieved and flown back to Washington without incident. By the time the team members arrived back in Washington, media interest in the mission had faded from view. Dr.Foster arranged for a private meeting with the President's National Security Advisor and in the latter's office orally communicated to him the details of what the team had discovered. With considerable apprehension, he gave his justification for keeping the discovery secret and for thoroughly destroying the wreckage. Much to Foster's relief, the presidential adviser agreed with his decision and told Foster he saw no reason to inform any other person. Some things, he noted, are better left secret.

The only problem now was what to tell Congressman Carpenter. The need to retain his good will was just as great as ever. After explaining to the Secretary of Defense and the Secretary of the Navy on the urgency of his plan, the National Security Advisor obtained their agreement to christen the next navy missile destroyer the USS Winston Carpenter. Theoretically, the Carpenter so honored was the late Captain Winston Carpenter, but Congressman Carpenter's association with his late father's bravery was stressed in all of the Pentagon's publicity on the subject. Happily, Congressman Carpenter can always be relied upon to throw his powerful support behind any Pentagon proposal for expensive new weapon's programs.

The Sterling Prize

Rutgard Sterling became one of the wealthiest men in the world through his invention of the formula that turns women's hair permanently blonde. From a tiny garage workshop near Stockholm, Sweden, he built up a giant manufacturing empire with factories all around the globe. Because of the strong and continuous demand for the product, his plants all operated at full capacity.

At length, Sterling decided it was time for him to retire. He was an orphan, had never married and had no known relations. This caused widespread speculation as to what would become of his wealth once he departed this world. There was great anticipation in Swedish political circles over the prospect of acquiring the Sterling fortune and using it to fiancé many desired but unimplemented programs.

Sterling had for many years engaged in a bitter dispute with the Swedish tax authorities of the government tax imposed on his product, which was taxed as a luxury rather than as what Sterling considered it to be a pharmaceutical product. For this reason, he determined that not even the smallest fragment of his wealth would ever fall into the greedy clutches of the government. Employing the best lawyers in Europe for the purpose, he had them design a philanthropic organization bearing his name with a structure so foolproof that every legal or administrative effort by the

Swedish government to alter its provisions was straightway rebuffed by the Swedish courts.

Into this foundation, Sterling put his entire fortune. Now he faced a problem. All of the logical humanitarian missions for such an institution had already been taken. Andrew Carnegie had already financed all the public libraries that were desired; the Rockefeller had already provided all of the medical research projects necessary. Sterling then recalled Alfred Nobel, the famed Swedish inventor of dynamite. Nobel had donated the bulk of his vast fortune to provide for prizes to be awarded individuals for their outstanding contributions to humanity. This gave Sterling an idea.

The problem with the Nobel Peace Prize, as Sterling saw it, while it rewarded a few admittedly outstanding individuals; it left the great bulk of mankind feeling worse about themselves. For example, while only a handful of physicists around the world could be logically considered as eligible for the annual Nobel prize in physics and only one actually win it, scores in every country would be left disappointed. Sterling concluded that to help remedy the problem; his foundation would award prizes each year in all the prominent areas of human endeavor to the individual whose performance or achievements had been the worst. Taking physics, for example, many physicists in every nation had come up lacking and might be considered, and the really incompetent ones would receive needed recognition.

Each year the annual award of the Sterling prizes was awaited with even greater anticipation than that of the Nobel prizes. The cash award in each case was so great that the fortunate recipient would become fabulously wealthy. Little wonder that when the panel selecting the winners gathered in Stockholm, the event was covered by hundreds of journalists.

Naturally there was some debate over the choices. The award of the prize for the worst political judgment to the president of a once great power.He had destroyed the wealth and population of his country by embarking on a series of unnecessary and disastrous wars was attacked. The choice as was attacked as rewarding the wrong individual by those who argued it should have gone to the monarch who ordered the abolition of all alcoholic drinks at the start of a major war, although his government was dependent on the government tax on liquor provided almost all of his government's revenues. Similarly, the choice of the Hanson prize in economics was bitterly contested by those who argued to should have gone to the central banker who convinced his government to go off the gold standard and print whatever amount of paper currency was thought necessary and the other economist who succeeded in implementing a rigid series of price and wage controls to curtail inflation and then provided that it be enforced by asking the population to observe the honor system.

It is sad to think that Sterling's prize intended to help the progress of mankind became the cause of so much harm. The size of the annual awards was so great that individuals began to strive to achieve disastrous results in order to compete for it. Political leaders, who always had the propensity to make unwise decisions and introduce programs clearly flawed now tried harder to worsen their performance in office. Most business decisions represented a senseless investment of company capital. More and more pharmaceutical products not only had little prospect of being effective but usually carried with them a host of grave health threats.

In the wake of these developments, the economies of all nations in which potential Sterling prize winners resided plummeted. Unemployment soared, wages plunged, and most corporations declared bankruptcy. If Sterling had still been alive, there was some chance he might have stepped in and altered the charter of his organization. Unfortunately, he had passed away and so could longer be appealed to. The situation grew so grave that the leaders of the world's great powers gathered to discuss the problem and hopefully to solve it. An effort in all of their highest courts to break the Sterling will. Once again, the provisions approved by Sterling proved unchallengeable.

It was clear that extra-legal methods had to be employed. The G-7 members and NATO passed identical resolutions authorizing "the use of whatever means might be necessary" to deal with the problem." Under the leadership of the US, a joint task force was formed made up of Navy Seals, British Special Forces and French commandos. It was carried in ultra-fast American transports that were designed to elude radar. They arrived in Stockholm on the eve of the meeting of the panel chosen to select the year's winners of the Sterling prize. He team took them into custody and dispatched them to the remote South Atlantic island of St. Helena, where they were given every possible comfort but barred from leaving or communicating with the outside world. Thus, with the panel unable to announce the prize winners, interest in pursuing s prize would decline and the world return to normal.

Alas, this brilliant plan failed. Unknown to the nations of the world, a secret codicil in Sterling's will provided that in case the panel was unable to meet for any reason, a substitute panel would meet secretly in Copenhagen, Denmark and designate that year's Sterling Prize winners. When the panel announced its choices, the world was astounded both that the brilliant effort to silence the panel had failed and the names of the winners. The vast sum awarded annually would be shared this year by the world leaders who had thought it possible to curtail human avarice and stupidity somehow.

Mad Scientist

From his earliest years, Chesterfield Cooper knew what his life's ambition would be. Let the other little boys prattle on about becoming a policeman, a fireman or a jet pilot. He knew he was going to be a mad scientist. Naturally his parents were naturally appalled when they learned his ambition. When they found that he had pasted a large posture depicting Dr. Frankenstein to his bedroom wall that they determined, action had to be taken. His father, a prominent Wall Street broker, took Cooper with him to his office, hoping to interest the boy in finance. The elder Cooper was pleased by his son's avid interest until he learned the reason. The boy wanted to learn how to manipulate the stock market to secure sufficient funding for his work as a mad scientist.

His mother now tried her turn at diverting him from his obsession. A gynecologist, she took him with her to the hospital, think that his interest in science might incline him to pursue medicine as a career. Alas. All Cooper was interested in was how medical science might be used as a starting point for research by a mad scientist. His desperate parents took him to one after another child psychologist and even to two psychiatrists. His was given numerous IQ and psychology tests. All the findings were the same. The boy was extremely intelligent and perfectly normal except for that one peculiar obsession. They usually recommended that the parents relax and give him time to grow out of it. One prominent, Viennese trained psychiatrist suggested that the parents remove the poster of Dr. Frankenstein and replace it with one of Louis Pasteur. However, the normally obedient child threw such a tantrum that they decided it was better to return Dr. Frankenstein's posture to its position on the wall.

As he grew older, Cooper learned to conceal his ambition. It was not from concern over antagonizing people but rather because it might impede the pursuit of his career goal. His high grades enabled him to gain admission to Harvard, where he took a double major in chemistry and physics. During the summer, rather than relaxing at his parent's beach home or taking a job as a counselor at a summer camp, as so many of his class-mates did, he took college courses in physics. He believed that to be a successful mad scientist it was necessary to be well trained in physics as well as in chemistry and biology.

Cooper graduated from Princeton at the age off nineteen. His parents were pleased when he applied and was accepted to continue on at Harvard for a graduate degree. They, fortunately, were unaware that his decision was due to the belief that no one will pay any attention to a mad scientist who does not affix the title of "Doctor" before his name. Whatever illusions they might have had that he had changed his ambition were cruelly shattered when he legally changed his last name from Cooper to Xorba. "Cooper," he explained when they pressed him for the reason, "Is inappropriate for a mad scientist, whereas Dr. Xorba carried with it all the right implications. He saw no reason to mention that he had also considered changing his first name at the same time, but had decided against it because most people do not know or care what a mad scientist's first name is. He cited as his rational that he had never heard any mention of Dr. Frankenstein's first name.

Xorba received his Ph.D. degree in biology, and then took a relatively low-paid job at the Massachusetts Institute of Technology as a lecturer in biology. His aim was not to perfect his teaching skills or his expertise in biology, of which he was already unusually proficient, but to informally acquire the knowledge of physics he would have obtained if his doctoral studies had been in that field. Four years later, he left MIT, although he had been pressed to remain on as an assistant professor. He then took a highly paid position as a senior researcher with a large pharmaceutical company in New Jersey. His parents were overjoyed, thinking that their eccentric son had finally grown up.

Little did they know. Upon saving up as much as he thought needed to achieve his ambition he resigned, again ignoring pleas from his employers to remain on. He purchased a dilapidated farm in an isolated corner of upper New York State and refurbished the barn, transforming it into a suitable facility to house a research laboratory. Sparing no expense, he installed in it all the equipment and supplies he might need and then set about his work.

To be a successful mad scientist, it is necessary to have accomplished some highly sensational research. He carefully considered all of the possible projects he might pursue and decided upon the most suitable. After four years of four years of sixteen an hour work, with nary an hour off to relax, he perfected his discovery. It was a transmitter with two terminals, which projected from one to the other a high frequency beam. Because of the particular parts within the terminals, most of which had been hand crafted by Dr. Xorba, the ray had the unique quality of being able to switch the head of one living organism onto the body of another.

Dr. Xorba prepared carefully for the announcement of his discovery. He waited for a stormy night, with lots of abundant thunder, believing that this atmospheric condition was appropriate if not necessary for an announcement by a mad scientist. After a few days wait the weather cooperated, and Dr. Xorba gave his presentation to a hall packed with representatives of the media and the scientific community. The high point of his presentation came when he raised the curtain and revealed the two transmitters and caged between them a mouse and a monkey. Turning on the transmitters, the beam sped between the two transmitters and instantaneously the head of the mouse appeared on the monkey's body and the head of the monkey on the mouse's torso. Both heads were alive and made their sounds expressing their surprise and alarm over the change in bodies.

Dr. Xorba settled back to await the expected shouts of fear and rage which customarily follow a mad scientist's announcement. None came. Obviously, he thought they were too shocked to speak. He left the hall and returned to his hotel, confident that the expected reaction would not be long in coming. Poor Dr. Xorba. The next morning when he eagerly searched the newspapers and watched the TV news show for the torrent of abuse and rage against him he expected to receive he was cruelly. disappointed. Not only was he not threatened with lynching nor even with being ridden out of town on a rail. To his shock, no one mentioned the horror of his invention. Instead, he was praised by the entire scientific community for inventing a device which might provide life and health to individuals with bodies racked by such diseases as cancer and stroke. Now, thanks to Dr. Xorba, their heads could be switched to the bodies of individuals who had been killed by injuries to the head.

Dr. Xorba was so depressed by this failure that although he did not normally drink, he got himself drunk and remained in that state for almost a week. A lesser man would have been crushed, but not Dr. Xorba. "After all," he told himself, "Success does not always come at the first try>" He girded his loins and returned to his research. He was even more optimistic about his eventual success than before, notwithstanding, the discouraging treatment he received as a "boon to all mankind" and the many offers, all of which he rudely rejected, from donors anxious to finance his research.

. This time it took him six years to complete the project. Having learned from his earlier experience that the weather was not an important factor in the reaction to a mad scientist's announcement, he did not bother to wait for a night with thunder and lightning. His second presentation was attended by an even larger audience that before, such was his fame.

To the packed hall, Dr. Xorba announced that he had modified his transmitters so that they could now change one living organism into another. To gasps of awe and disbelief, he raised the curtain behind him to reveal a rabbit and a single transmitter. He then turned on the transmitter and the directed the beam at the rabbit. It instantly was transformed into a man-killing alligator which Dr. Xorba had not restricted in any way to heighten the shock effect if it pursued any of the audience. Unfortunately, Dr. Xorba had neglected to order that the rabbit not be fed. The alligator, having a full stomach from the rabbit's meal was sluggish and not desposed to attack any of the spectators.

The reaction of the audience to Dr. Xorba's presentation was, like the previous one, one of shocked silence. This time he was prepared but not discouraged. He went back to his hotel confident that in the morning he would be hated as the worst mad scientist ever known. Poor Dr. Xorba. When he awakened the next morning and learned the public reaction, he realized he was a total failure. Every newspaper in the country hailed his achievement. The "New York Times," not known for hyperbole, referred to him in a full-page report on its front page as "the greatest living scientist in the world." The only critical comment came at the end of one paper's story. It which noted that there had been some feeling that Dr. Xorba had used sensationalist tactics by placing a ferocious alligator on the stage in an effort to impress the audience with his admittedly historic discovery.

There was no doubt that Dr. Xorba would be awarded a Nobel Prize for his discovery. The only question was whether it would be in biology or in physics. Unable to decide, the panel solved their dilemma by awarding the famed scientist one in each field, the only person in the history to receive simultaneously two Nobel Prizes, Dr. Xorba knew when he was beaten. It was hard for a person of Dr. Xorba's relatively tender age to admit that his life had been a total failure, but he was man enough to face the truth.

Xorba was indeed a broken man. He retired to a tropical island in the Caribbean where he still resides. He has changed his name back to Chesterfield Cooper and is addressed fondly as "Chet" by the many beautiful women who come as visitors to the luxury resort at which he lives and endeavor to enjoy the excitement of going to bed with the world's most famous scientist. He sits on the beach all day, enjoying the sun and the ocean. Since he is fabulously wealthy, he has no financial concerns. Three new planned developments in the US have been named after him, and his face appears on the postage of one African nation. There is no doubt that he will be similarly honored on an American postage stamp when he dies, the delay arising only because of the US tradition of not honoring a living person on a postage stamp.

The case of poor Dr. Xorba, or as he is now Dr. Cooper, illustrates the futility of trying to become a mad scientist. What good are wealth, fame and beautiful women if you are a failure in your lifelong ambition? Thus, it is with human nature.

Avoid The Fire

When Harvey Brownstown was a child, the movies he saw depicting the courage and glamour of the Marines made an indelible impression on him. Therefore, when shortly after graduating from high school he happened to pass the local recruiting office, he was unable to resist the call to arms made to him by the poster in the shop window. It showed a handsome Marine dressed in dress blues, with a beautiful girl embracing him warmly. The legend at the poster's top screamed "BE A MAN! ENLIST TODAY!" The legend at the bottom read "JOIN THE MARINES! MAKE YOURSELF, YOUR GIRL AND YOUR COUNTRY PROUD!"

Without another thought, Harvey entered the office and enlisted in the United States Marine Corps. In a few days he was sent off with some other enlistees to the Marine training camp at Parris Island, South Carolina. There he was placed in a training platoon with some thirty other new recruits and subjected to thirteen weeks of harsh treatment inflicted on the fledgling Marines. Revilie before damn, twenty-mile marches with full packs, and late night exercises were all part of the norm. The stated goal of this purposeful brutality was to break them down in order to refashion them into Marines.

Four members of Harvey's platoon were "washed out" of the platoon for various reasons and returned to civilian life. Harvey privately hoped that he would be added to this list. However, as much as he had come to despise boot camp, he was even more afraid of almost succeeding and being obliged to repeat the entire thirteen week course again. Accordingly, he managed to just make the grade and, graduating with the others posted to a Marine rifle company.

In his new assignment, Harvey was scarcely more satisfied than he had been in boot camp. The discipline was still harsh, the "gung ho" Marine Corps spirit foolish to a young man who had always prided himself on thinking for himself.

Lying exhausted on his hard cot in the barracks, he morosely cursed the fate that had brought him into the Marine Corps. If only, he thought, he might somehow be returned to civilian life, he would never seek after military life again.

Three months after joining the rifle company, it was assigned to the military force the United States was assembling to invade one of the Caribbean islands whose authoritarian government had been highlighted in the American media as being uncaring about the needs of its population. Thrown into the assault on the island capital, Harvey's platoon lost more than a quarter of the men killed or injured. Harvey prudently lagged behind in the attack, thereby avoiding the enemy fire until the engagement had been won.

Returning home, the company was given liberty. Harvey dressed himself in the blue dress uniform and inspected himself in the mirror. Yes, he thought, he did resemble the Marine he had seen on that recruiting poster. Surely, he would have no difficulty in attracting the beautiful woman who story had it, fell for any young Marine they saw.

Once again, military life proved to be a distinct disappointment. He did not attract a crowd of beautiful women, not even one. He sat at the bar, sadly nursing a drink and observing what went on. There many beautiful single women in the bar, most searching for male companionship. Quite naturally, rather than selecting a Marine private, they wisely chose to attract the attention of the well dressed, well heeled civilians, who could provide more attractive entertainment.

Harvey returned to his barracks a sadder but wiser man. He became increasingly bitter and refused to speak to anyone unless forced to do so. Although he did not like liquor particularly, he got himself drunk one night at the PX and suffered from a horrible hangover for two days. At last, he resolved to make the best of a bad situation. He could not get out of the Marines until he completed his three-year hitch. During that time, he would do his best to be the best Marine possible, to live up to the ideals of the Marine Corps.

In a few more months, Harvey's company was again sent into combat, once again to remove another Latin American government the administration in Washington decided had failed to meet the standards urged by the United Nations. Once again, Harvey's company was in the van of the attack. When the order to charge was given, Harvey sprang forward, rifle in hand, yelling to the men behind him "Follow me!"

The courageous but foolish Harvey fell to the ground in a heap, his body smashed by seven enemy bullets. After the battle had been won, Harvey's body was collected and shipped home in a body bag. A few months later, a new democratic regime took power in the country, and Harvey's company returned to the United States. A few weeks after their departure, the new government promptly annulled the new Constitution and returned to the ways of the previous regime.

Although it was too late to take advantage of it, in the last fleeting second of his life, as he was falling to the ground, Harvey learned something he should have known all his life. No matter how bad the situation is, do not try to change it if there is a substantial risk of simply making it worse. In other words, as the old proverb puts it, do not jump from the frying pan into the fire.

Follow The Rats

When the water reaches the gunnels, it's time to follow the rats off the sinking ship," is a frequently repeated expression. From the time he first heard it, Livingston Minor was curious about the accuracy of its description of rat judgment. He was the scion of a wealthy old Boston family. As the beneficiary of a large trust fund, he was able to purchase a townhouse in Boston's prestigious Back Bay Section and to hire a butler and cook to serve him. When he graduated from Princeton he opted not to join the family's private investment bank founded by his great grandfather, but instead to look into the behavior of rats.

Minor purchased a boarded up old warehouse and fitted it up as a laboratory. He then purchased ten rats from a laboratory animal supply company and subjected them to careful scruting. He found their behavior very similar to that of humans. Some were obviously possessed with more intelligence than others. They sometimes played with each other, sometimes got into spats, almost always enjoyed eating and had individual preferences with regard to which foods they found most desirable. Their sexual habits were similar, although the sexual activity of female rats was more closely related to the period of fertility than was the case with human females.

One problem was that Minor's objectivity in the pursuit of

knowledge became seriously compromised by his growing affinity for some of the rats. Several of the more intelligent began to recognize him and rushed eagerly to the front of their cages when they saw him approaching at the time he customarily fed them. Then one day he was startled when one of them brought over to him a piece of the cheese Minor had provided earlier in an apparent gesture to show his gratitude to Minor.

This was too much. Minor felt guilty treating the rats like mere animals. He promptly abandoned the project and sold the factory and its equipment. The rats he provided for at the family farm, building a rather luxurious rat house for them to live in and hiring one of the farm workers to look after their comfort. The rate enclosure was equipped with air conditioning to make them more comfortable in summer and with electric heating to protect them from the cold of winter.

Still, Minor remained curious about rats. Walking down the sidewalk of one Boston side street early one morning, he spied a rat keeping pace with him close to the buildings. The rat was obviously aware of his presence but showed no fear of him, all the while keeping him in constant sight., Minor was sure that if he had made a threatening move toward the rat, the rodent would flee to the safety of a hallway or sidewalk grate.

This could be the opportunity he sought. "Pardon me, sir," he said politely to the rat, "Do you have a moment for me to ask you a question?"

The rat stopped. "I'm afraid I'm in rather a hurry," it said. "I have a pressing engagement. But if you need to speak with me, I can meet you here tomorrow at the same time." The rat then set off again at his previous pace.

Minor recognized the futility of trying to press the rat now. Accordingly, he went about his business, but the following day came to the designated meeting spot. Sure enough, he found the rat awaiting his arrival. "Thanks for meeting me," he began. May I ask you a few questions?"

"Shoot," the rat answered, "But please try to make it brief. I'm afraid I have another business meeting today."

Minor quoted the old saying about rats leaving sinking ships and asked if it was true. "I'm afraid I can't help you there," the rat answered. "I've never been on a ship. I don't know how I'd act if the shipping, but I probably would get off it. That's just common sense."

Seeing Minor's disappointment, the rat suggested," I do have some friends who live along the waterfront. Possibly one or two of them would be able to answer your question." They arranged to meet again the next evening, when the rat would take Minor to the waterfront and introduce him to his friends.

The rat proved to be as good as his word. He introduced minor to several rats who had knowledge of the subject. The most helpful to Minor was an old rat who had spent many years at sea on a variety of merchant vessels. He assured Minor that any intelligent rat would leave a sinking ship in enough time not to go down with it. He added that based on his long experience, most seafaring rats were smart enough to make that judgment at the proper time.

Over the course of time, Minor was introduced to numerous rats by his rat mentor, whose name turned out to be Butterworth. The latter was quite prominent in rat business circles and a leader in the charitable organizations that provided assistance to the city's large indigent rat population. Minor joined in to assist Butterworth in these activities. He took particular satisfaction from his role in dispensing Thanksgiving and Christmas dinners to poor rats who often did not have enough to eat.

During his work with the rats, Minor learned a lot about them. He found that some of the popular expressions relating to rats were downright wrong. For example, rats to not engage in a "rat Race" any more than humans do in a "human race>" He learned that most are highly social, helping each other to escape from traps and sharing favored items of food. He met one who had been honored on the battlefield for alerting troops about the presence of landmines.

It is sad to think that Minor's involvement with rats brought about his untimely demise Minor and several rat associates were in an abandoned factory, concentrating on bringing a warm, nutritious meal to one parent rat families, when the doors and windows of the building were tightly sealed. Unknown to Minor, the factory owners had become seriously concerned by the large amount of rat droppings found in the plant and had engaged a leading firm of pest exterminators to deal with the problem.

The plant was large, and and believed to harbor many rats. Therefore, believed to inhabit it, a new and highly toxic gas was forced into the sealed structure. The next morning, the windows and doors were opened, and the plant aired out. Too late! Entering the building, the factory managers found on the floor amid the bodies of many dead rats the remains of Livingston Minor.

Everyone involved, the pest exterminating the factory owners, the city authorities and Minor's own family agreed that it would be better if the news of the tragedy was kept from the public. The rat carcasses were disposed of in the city facility used for the purpose. Minor's family was planning to bury his remains in the family burial plot. However, when Minor's will was read, it stated he wished in the event of his death to be laid to rest among his rat friends.

Today, Minor sleeps in eternal rest along with his friends. We can't be sure, but it is very likely that if he could smile, there would be an eternal smile on Livingston Minor's face. Few among us can honestly say we have lived as worthwhile a life as Minor or have accomplished so much good. And, of course, the ambition that set him on his life's course, to determine rather rats will really leave a sinking ship when the water reaches the gunnels, has been satisfied. The answer is absolutely yes. Beyond that, the average rat is smart enough to leave the ill-fated vessel at the most advantageous time to assure the most favorable chances of survival.

School Reform

When Connecticut, one of the richest states in the nation by virtue of its high average annual income, announced it was suffering from unprecedented financial pressures, it was clear that a series challenge faced the country. The primary cause was a steady and rapid rise in education costs, resulting in very sharp increases in local property taxes and a large outflow from the state treasury to the municipalities for educational purposes.

In desperation, the State Government took the usual course adopted in such circumstances; it formed a blue ribbon special committee to investigate the problem and provide a solution. All of its members were chosen from among the members of the Education Departments in the various schools rather than resorting to actual elementary and high school teachers who had practical experience in the matter. The committee held hears over a three month period, listening to testimony from education officials, various members of state and municipal government and the general public. It then held closed sessions for another two months drafting the joint report.

In its final version as submitted to the Governor of Connecticut included the customary three options. The first one was to simply cut the school day by fifty percent, thereby allowing a similar reduction in the salaries paid to teachers. The report noted that this option would undoubtedly engender a strong reaction on the part of the powerful teachers' unions and gave it short shrift.

The third option was to continue to fund education programs with no policy modifications. The financial shortfall would be covered by cutting or eliminating other government services, including police, sanitation and road construction and maintenance. This option had several advantages. Eliminating police forces would tend to increase the number and severity of clashes between the police and low- income urban areas, thereby improving the tempo of needed social change. Removing garbage trucks from the streets would help reduce traffic congestion and slightly shorten the driving time for most commuters. The reported pointed out a major disadvantage, that it would probably provoke such opposition among voters that it would lead to the ouster in the next election of most elected officials.

Thus, as is the case with all such commissions, it threw its weight behind the middle option. This involved shifting the school day from the customary daylight hours to after dark. School buses would begin picking up children for transport to schools at eight p.m. in the evening and deposit them at their schools about nine p.m. The school day would end at three a.m., with the school buses picking them up at their schools and dropping them off at their homes about four p.m.

The great advantage of this option was that it would permit municipalities to rent out the public school buildings during the day for use as office space and for commercial establishments. The change would provide a large new source of income for educational purposes and for funding other needed programs. There was little doubt that option two was the best choice. After some debate, the educational reform bill as it was labeled was approved by the State Legislature and signed by the governor.

The shift in school hours went ahead with few problems. Mothers with children at kindergarten age or older were freed of the need to provide daytime babysitting. Child psychologists confirmed that the change eliminated the problem of "latchkey children returning to homes in which no parent or guardian was available because at four p.m. they would simply throw themselves into bed to sleep rather than getting into trouble. Most parents welcomed the new ease with which they could go out after eight p.m. without having to pay for babysitters. Doctors commended the move as reducing the threat of adult skin cancer because the school age children would never be in the sun.

Many commercial establishments reported profit gains from the school reform. Restaurants, movies, bars and bowling allies saw greatly increased use as parents could now go out more. Cosmetics firms had to modify their lipsticks, and other beauty supplies sold to teenage and sub-teen age girls so for use after dark rather than during the day, giving them the opportunity to revise their packages slightly and greatly increase their prices.

Admittedly there were a few problems, A few students strongly attacked the change and threatened to call student strikes. The school authorities, concerned, consulted with child psychologists and successfully overcame student resistance through the new "make the student feel good program" This involved basing test scores and grades not on performance but on student popularity. All students rated each other from the most popular down to the least popular student, with highest grades awarded to the most popular.

The resentment aroused on the part of the least popular students, many of them nerds or academically advantaged in more classical academic fields, over the lower grades they received was easily appeased. They were given the privilege of selecting which movies the classes were shown throughout their class time. While officially designed to enhance the students' knowledge of the subject, the movies had the additional advantage of allowing the teachers, most of whom had taken daytime jobs, to sleep at their desks.

Connecticut's school reform plan proved so successful that it was quickly adopted by forty-eight of the other states. Only Alaska did not follow suit. There the Eskimos successfully opposed it, arguing that they required the assistance of their children at night to catch the seals, vital as a source of food and pelts.

Of course, the reform resulted in occasional minor difficulties which were quickly overcome. When the decline in the scores in the tests administered every few years to all students in mathematics and writing skills led to this country being ranked one hundred and sixty-seventh among the hundred and sixty-seven nations covered by the survey, this was easily handled. The tests were given to a representative sample of the student population to establish its suitability and then modified to insure that at least eighty percent of all those taking the test in the United States would achieve the desired level of achievement. Education experts and government officials are confident that when the test are administered next year, the United States will regain one hundred and sixty-eighth place in the national rankings.

The story of the educational reforms is one to make all Americans proud. It shows that through cooperation and common effort by parents, students, educators and government officials, nothing is impossible. If we can all resolve to keep on this path, there is no doubt that the United States will reach even greater stature as the most admired nation and accepted pathfinder for the World.

The Probe

The bystanders who happened to witness Mr. Avery Proctor struck down and killed by a speeding car at 9:23 in the morning of Tuesday, April 23rd while crossing Duke Street in Alexandria, Virginia, agreed that Proctor's death was accidental. Authorities, investigating the death, reached the same conclusion. The fact that the motorist responsible had not stopped or subsequently reported the incident to the police was not regarded as particularly important. The accident had occurred during rush hour when most of the drivers were hurrying to their jobs in the nation's capital. Naturally, it was assumed, they would not wish to be late arriving at their office.

Only Ashley Proctor, Avery's twin sister, knew his death had not been an accident. Despite the difference in sex, the twins looked remarkably alike. On that particular morning, both had been wearing tan trench coats and dark, felt hats pulled down over the brow. It was not difficult for Ashley to conclude that those responsible for murdering Avery had mistaken him for her.

As a senior official of the Central Intelligence Agency, Ashley was aware that she was always a prime target for foreign adversaries. Her skillful performance of her duties made her a lightning rod for the country's many adversaries. Virtually every success the agency had scored in recent years could be laid at her door; most of its failures resulted from senior government officials ignoring her recommendations.

It took no time for Ashley to resolve to devote all her energy to finding and eliminating those responsible for her brother's murder. Not only had the twins been very close, but she herself had been the intended target of the planned assassination. She straightaway took extended leave from the CIA.

This was not as easy as might be thought. In order to protect the personal identity of its clandestine operatives, their submission of formal leave requests was officially frowned upon. Normally this caused no difficulty. The exception was one Tuesday just two days before Christmas, when all of the agents decided separately to take the day off. This happened to coincide with a surprise visit to CIA Headquarters by the President, who intended personally to congratulate the members of the Clandestine Service for their heroic efforts.

The President arrived at the Headquarters Building to find it totally empty, except for one agent who had come to the office to seek refuge from the unpleasant music being played in his home by his son, home from college. Fortunately, the agent had the presence of mind to whisper to the President that Agency scientists had come up with a working cloak of invisibility. Coupled with a wink, this convinced the Chief Executive that his intelligence agency was even more effective than he had supposed, and he returned to the White House happy about his visit.

As a senior member of the clandestine service, Ashley had many well-placed contacts around the world, both official and unofficial, whom she could rely upon to do her a favor. She tried all of them, without result. None had the slightest knowledge of any plot to assassinate her.

Ashley was not fazed by this. She recalled attending a briefing of senior officials in the bowels of the CIA Headquarters. The Agency scientists had begun by reporting that their efforts to invent a time machine, stimulated by reports that the Soviet KGB was investigating the possibility, had resulted in the conclusion that this was not technically feasible. However, as an offshoot to the research, the scientists had produced a time probe, whereby events in the recent past could be watched in the Agency. Ashley determined to use the time probe to ascertain the parties responsible for her brother's murder.

All of Ashley's training and experience led her to conclude this was no time to wait. That very night, shortly after dusk, she arrived at the Agency gate. The guards on duty knew her by sight and waved her in, with only a cursory look at her identity badge. Once in the Headquarters, she descended into the bowels of the building. At the lowest level, she reached the door of the chamber which housed the probe.

The door was locked and sealed, but Ashley was skilled at breaking and entering without leaving a trace. Inside the chamber, she seated herself at the console directing the probe. The controls were well-marked and easily comprehensible. Ashley turned the machine on and steered the probe back to the place, date and exact minute of her brother's death. She had no doubt that she could spot the murder car, stop the frame, and identify the driver of the vehicle.

Unfortunately, what came into view on the console screen was not Duke Street in Alexandria, Virginia, but Elm Street in Dallas, Texas on November twenty-second, 1963. Startled, Ashley saw the motorcade carrying President John Kennedy, his wife Jacqueline and Vice President Lyndon Johnson precede to the Texas School Book Depository Building, from which rifle shots rang out. She saw the President, clearly wounded in the head, slump down, and the car sped off.

"My God!" she exclaimed, almost hysterical. "So that's it. The failed assassination plot against me was part of a larger plot which succeeded in killing the President."

Ashley, of course, could not have known that the probe was not functioning properly. The Iranian Government in retaliation for CIA efforts to cripple the Iranian nuclear weapons program had succeeded in inserting a computer virus into the computer operating the probe. The virus caused the probe dials to register incorrect dates and places from the information fed into its controls. She further was unaware that the probe emitted a low frequency electric wave, which affected the electrical functions of the brain of any human in close proximity.

Completely muddled by what she had seen, Ashley turned off the probe, left the chamber, carefully sealed the door lock, and made her way out of the Headquarters unobserved. Back home, she fell into a fitful sleep. She awakened the next morning with the problem solved by her subconscious mind. She would go back to the Agency and take another look at the Kennedy assassination. By shifting the coverage slightly, she could examine the top floor of the Texas School Book Depository building and confirm the identity of the shooter, either Lee Harvey Oswald or some other person. Determining the identity of the assassin would go a long way in aiding her to identify those responsible for her brother's murder.

That evening, just after dusk, Ashley approached the gate leading into the CIA Headquarters. The scene that greeted her was very different from what it had been on the previous evening. In addition to the customary couple of Agency uniformed guards, a large number of troops posted at close intervals along the Agency perimeter, all grim-faced and holding automatic weapons at the ready, stood watch. She spotted an Agency guard standing awkwardly to one side and approached him. She had seen him occasionally and sometimes had exchanged a few polite remarks with him.

"What's the trouble?" she asked in a low voice.

"Everyone's flapping," he answered. "Word is that the giant secret computer they have in the basement exploded. Seems the Chinese or the Russians hacked into it and gave it an instruction to self-destruct."

Ashley thanked the guard and turned away. She knew when

she was licked. With all obvious methods of finding her brother's killer stymied, she ended her leave and returned to duty at the Agency. She has since been promoted and is widely rumored in Washington political circles to be next in line for the post of Agency Deputy Director.

It is not to be thought, however, that Ashley has given up all efforts to find her attempted assassin. The day before she ended her vacation, she drove to a public library in West Virginia and used the computer there to write and then print a letter. Wearing gloves to avoid leaving fingerprints, she mailed it off to California.

Ashley knew, of course, that it would risk her future at the Agency if she went public with the fact that her brother's death was a failed effort to assassinate her and that this was intricately linked to the Kennedy assassination. To have done so would have placed her at odds with the official report of the Warren Commission, which the Agency would find too controversial. To an agent of her intelligence and ability and keen knowledge of how to motivate people, a good alternative was available. Now each day she waits to see what the recipient of her letter, film director Oliver Stone, will reveal in his widely-anticipated new expose of the conspiracy behind Kennedy's death.

The Submersible

For six days a week, George Stevenson did the same thing every day at the same hour for the same length of time. The seventh day, Sunday, he rested. Most of what he did was totally useless, and George was well aware of this fact. He followed his schedule because it gave his life the order it required. Without it, he knew, he would be lost. It was all he could do under the circumstances to keep himself sane.

It is not a simple matter for someone to keep from yielding to despair when living alone in a windowless metal enclosure only thirty feet long by five feet wide. Add to that the fact that he knew he was living more than a hundred feet below the level of the sea. If his submersible developed a leak, he would quickly drown. And George had been living alone in that submersible for some three and a half years.

George's fate was even worse. He could calculate almost exactly the day of his death. It would come when he exhausted his food supply. He would have to come to the surface, whether the living conditions were capable of sustaining life or not. By his estimate, he had another two years to live. He could increase it somewhat by reducing his consumption of food, but he had already done so once. He was now always hungry, looking forward eagerly to the next small meal. A further reduction of food would make his life unbearable. It was better, he thought, to sacrifice the few days or weeks more he might have been able to eke out from extending it through a period of near-starvation.

The daily ritual was always the same. He awakened at six, exercised on his treadmill for an hour, and then had breakfast. At nine, he would carefully check his remaining food supply. He did not have to worry about air to breath or water to drink. The submersible was equipped with equipment that could break down the ocean water surrounding him into its individual components, yielding pure oxygen and potable water.

George's schedule allotted an hour for reading, then a skimpy lunch. The choice of dishes for all of his meals was quite narrow: cans of fruit, cans of main courses such as spaghetti, franks and beans or stewed chicken and canned crackers in lieu of bread. His f favorite dishes were the canned applesauce and the canned chicken. George heated the cans in boiling water and then emptied the contents onto his plate. The only thing he actually made from scratch was his beverage, coffee, tea or cocoa. Naturally, George was tired by the monotony of his diet and longed for the foods he once enjoyed, cake, fresh bread and Oriental food.

After lunch, George would spend a few hours reading. The submersible was stocked with a large library of books, all available for reading via his computer screen. Virtually every American novel published in the last hundred years was included, as well as a good collection of reference works and some foreign classics. His eyesight had deteriorated since he was in the submersible, and he had no way of obtaining corrective glasses. After a few hours of reading, his eyes would start to bother him. He would stop and take a nap.

When he awakened, George would have a light dinner choosing from the same menu as before. Then would come the treat of the day. He would select a movie from the large assortment of films available to him, and then turn in. Under the circumstances, it is not strange that he preferred to watch comedies to dramas.

Sundays were the best day I the week. He would permit himself to watch two movies, one in the afternoon and another in the evening. He also had in his larder a small quantity of "special treats," that had been included for morale purposes. There were small quantities of canned cranberry sauce, which he enjoyed with chicken, some packages of chocolate, and several cases of small champagne bottles, for celebrations. George would select one of these treats to make something of a celebration for his Sunday dinner. On the Thanksgiving Days and Christmas Days he had spent on the submersible, he permitted himself one of the treats at each meal.

As unhappy as he was over his existence, George knew that he was very lucky. Just about all of the people he had known before boarding the submersible, just about all of the people then living, were now dead. Frozen by the awful cold. George owed his survival to luck and to the fact that he had worked as a nautical engineer.

After prolonged debate, the American government finally accepted the report of its scientists that the Earth was about to experience a period of decreased solar activity. Temperatures would fall so low that all living things on the surface of the planet would be destroyed. Immediately, frantic efforts were made to ensure the survival of the human race. Similar attempts were made by other great powers. Obviously, provision could be made for only a handful to survive. Two courses of action were suggested, one was to tunnel deep into the earth in the hope that the intervening layers of soil would provide insulation from the freezing temperatures on the surface. The other was to construct a fleet of submersible vessels which would allow people in them to survive far enough below the surface of the sea, where the water would provide insulation.

As a maritime engineer, George was employed in helping to construct the submersibles. Each one was designed to enable two adults, one male and one female, and two children to survive in them for three years. The adults would be of child-bearing age, and it was hoped that two children would be born before the submersible was forced to come to the surface. In addition to the necessary provisions, each submersible was stocked with a supply of seeds which, it was hoped, could be planted on land. Since no livestock could be carried on the submersibles, the survivors would have to become vegetarians, other than possibly catching such marine life that had managed to survive in the ocean.

When the tunneling effort encountered difficulties, priority was given to the submersibles program. The initial projected number of five hundred thousand was doubled. Unfortunately, after the designs had been finalized, and some seven hundred thousand of the craft constructed, a review of the design plans revealed a disastrous flaw in the calculations. The mechanism for providing breathable air from sea water did function as projected. However, the daily maximum rate of oxygen supply was only sufficient to sustain one adult, not two adults and two children as had been envisaged.

A very large number of people had sought space on one of the submersibles as the only chance of escaping death from the cold. To handle the choice fairly, most of the slots were allotted in equal numbers to adults of childbearing age who met extremely high health and intelligence requirements. Even with the pool of possible selectees thus limited, each slot could have been filled many hundreds of thousands over. Once it was revealed that the submersibles could carry only a single adult, the number of people interested dropped precipitously; few looked forward to spending years alone in a small vessel in the ocean depths.

Even so, George was fortunate to be awarded a place. He was aided by having access to a small pool of slots reserved for individuals working on the program. Naturally, a much larger special allotment was assigned to prominent government officials and their friends and relatives. There were even unconfirmed rumors that a special ten-person submersible had been constructed for the use of the President, his family and escorting Secret Service agents and press advisors.

George's initial relief at gaining one of the prized slots quickly turned to unhappiness after spending six months in the craft. The cramped quarters, the monotony of the diet and, worst of all, the isolation, ate at him. Often he thought that the people who had been left behind to die in the cold were perhaps the lucky ones.

One day, as George was just finishing a lunch of franks and beans, with very little meat, he heard a violent pounding at the front of the submersible. He rushed to the sonar apparatus and studied the screen. On two previous occasions he had heard similar sounds; consulting the sonar had revealed the noise was caused by large maritime creatures hitting the ship. He was startled to find the sonar set displaying a figure at the bow of the submersible unlike that of a whale or giant squid. Instead, it seemed to resemble a human.

The submersible had in its bow a single opening in the heavy metal outer shell, a tiny porthole. Normally, it was covered with a heavy metal porthole cover to lessen the possibility of the porthole glass breaking and water flooding into the submersible. George hastily unlocked the porthole cover, opened it and peered through the heavy glass. The vessel was at so great a depth that almost no light penetrated that far down.

George was amazed to see staring at him from the other side of the porthole a human face. He thought it must have been his imagination and stared again. There was no doubt. It was a human face. George was not certain if the creature, man or fish could see into the submersible. He stepped back and waved and smiled, hoping to establish communication. He thought he saw it wave back before it turned and swam away.

As he sat down, trying to decide exactly what he had seen and its significance to him, he recalled something he had overheard as he was boarding the submersible. Forced to recognize the limited prospects of success from the submersible program or the tunneling effort, the government had shifted its attention to DNA experimentation, hoping to so modify the DNA of cloned human specimens to permit them to survive living in the ocean bottoms. He now realized that whether he survived or not, whether life on land was now possible thanks to renewed solar activity, the role of mankind as he had known it was finished. Man would no longer be the dominant species on Earth.

Halloween

It was Halloween, the one night each year when the shades of the damned buried in Boot Hill are permitted to walk the earth. Black Jack McBride, widely rumored to have killed fourteen men, not counting Indians or Mexicans, was seated disconsolately on a tombstone, smoking a cigarette. On his chest, the wounds of the shotgun blast from the sheriff who had killed him were visible in all their glory. Smoking a cigarette each Halloween was about the only pleasure he had left. Fortunately, when he was shot by that sheriff, he had the cigarettes in his pocket. They were, therefore, available now to his ghost. Unfortunately, the stock of cigarettes was not being replaced, and he calculated he had only enough for a few more years.

He heard a sound and looked up. It was the ghost of Frank Hollister. Around his neck, the marks of the rope with which he had been hanged were clearly visible. Black Jack shuddered. Of all the damned souls who arose from Boot Hill on Halloween, the most annoying was Hollister. He was always complaining, not about being hanged but about his bungling the affair. He was fond of telling everyone about how he had murdered his wife and two stepsons to gain possession of the richest silver mine in Nevada. "If only," he kept repeating in a lachrymose voice, "I had used some of that silver to bribe the jury, I would never have been convicted."

Hollister stared enviously at Jack's cigarette. You're damned lucky to be able to smoke a cigarette," he said. "When they hanged me, I couldn't have anything I wanted on me. If I still had a soul, I'd cheerfully trade it to have a bottle of whisky in my pocket."

In an effort to shut him up, Black Jack regretfully offered Hollister one of his few reaming cigarettes. Hollister looked like he was about to resume his sad regrets when Black Jack was elated to see a third figure approach. It was the ghost of Injun Joe. He had been killed by numerous shots in his back, whose wounds formed a tight pattern.

"How," said Injun Joe, raising his right hand in greeting and looking for all the world to see like a cigar store Indian. "I see white man smoking cigarette. Can give one to Injun Joe?"

Injun Joe had actually attended a one-room log cabin school house for five years, thanks to the influence of his white father. When the latter had untimely died, complaints by the parents of the other students over having their children attend classes with an Indian had led to his expulsion, but not before he had acquired the ability to read, write and speak English reasonably well. Still, he believed he had to live up to the stereotype his name suggested.

On several previous Halloweens, the other shades of the damned souls buried in Boot Hill had discussed Injun Joe's case. They all wondered how he had ended up a ghost, given his lack of serious crimes while alive. As Injun Joe explained it, he had been shot as a result of a misunderstanding with a bartender who thought he was attempting to take a bottle of whisky from the bar without paying for it. According to Injun Joe, he had been drunk at the time because of several drinks given him by other bar patrons anxious to see how many drinks were needed to get an Indian drunk. As a result of his inebriation, he admitted, he might have inadvertently not paid the right price for the bottle or indeed anything at all.

Remembering the Indian's sad story, Black Jack handed him a cigarette. "Thamk you," said Injun Joe, "I can really use a smoke," before realizing he had inadvertently stepped out of character. He relaxed when he saw that the others had apparently not noticed his slip. All three sat on their tombstones silently smoking. It was no longer fun, Black Jack thought, to be sprung from Boot Hill every Halloween and walk the earth. Living people no longer believed in ghosts. If anyone saw him from a distance, they thought he was a child in costume collecting his treat or trick candy. Up close, when they could see he was an adult, they would assume him to be someone going to a Halloween masquerade party.

Black Jack's sad reflections were interrupted by a flash of light and the appearance of a figure before him. It was a man, wearing a white robe, with a halo above his head and wings. In his left hand, he held a harp.

"Am I speaking to Black Jack McBride?" he asked politely.

"That's me," came back the answer. "Who are you?"

Permit me to introduce myself," the man said. "I am the angel Mordecai. I come to you with a very important message."

"What is it?" Black Jack asked. He was startled to think that an angel would have a message for him.

"You probably are not aware of it, being in Boot Hill that we are computerizing our records in Heaven. While imputing your information into the computer, it was discovered that an unfortunate administrative error was made. Instead of the fourteen individuals you are credited with killing, the correct number is four, and two of them were apparently cases of justifiable self defense."

"Does that mean I can get out of here?" Black Jack asked hopefully.

"I'm afraid not," came back the answer. "The error was purely an administrative one, not one of substance. "Still," the angel continued, we do feel we owe you a sincere expression of regret."

A lot of good that does me, Black Jack thought to himself. Then he was heartened when he heard Mordecai continue. "As a concrete token of our regret, henceforth your supply of cigarettes will automatically replenish itself."

"For a long time?" Black Jack asked eagerly.

"Oh, for all eternity."

There was another flash of light and the angel departed skyward. Black Jack reached into his pocket and gave Hollister and Injun Joe each another cigarette. They sat there smoking without speaking. Then Black Jack broke the silence, speaking more to himself than to the others. "For a shade living in Boot Hill," he said, "It's rather a nice present." The others nodded in agreement. It was the most pleasant Halloween any of them had had for a long time.

CPSIA information can be obtained at www.ICGtesting.com
Printed in the USA
LVOW08*1607240315

431819LV00002B/11/P